HOMER'S ODYSSEY

Homer's Odyssey SIMON ARMITAGE

faber and faber

First published in 2006
by Faber and Faber Limited
3 Queen Square London WC1N 3AU
This paperback edition published in 2007

Typeset by RefineCatch Limited, Bungay, Suffolk
Printed in England by T.J. International Ltd, Padstow, Cornwall

A CIP record for this book
is available from the British Library

ISBN 978-0-571-22936-9

10 9 8 7 6 5 4 3 2 1

INTRODUCTION

Twenty years have passed since Odysseus sailed away to wage war against the Trojans, leaving behind his beloved wife, Penelope, and Telemachus, their infant son. The conflict itself lasts for ten of those years, but another decade of strife awaits the victorious Odysseus as he hauls home towards his kingdom of Ithaca. The *Odyssey* is the story of that homeward journey, a journey which tests the resources and strength of its hero to breaking point. In his way stand cannibals and whirlpools, witches and ghosts, monsters and Gods. The battles he must win are battles of the body, the mind and the spirit. Homer's *Odyssey* forms part of the bedrock of all written art; one of the first ever works of literature, it is a triumph of intellectual, imaginative and technical genius. Ultimately, though, it is a story, and for all its evocation of the supernatural and the otherworldly, it is a story of humankind. At its heart is a family – a husband, wife and son – desperate to reunite and determined to survive.

This dramatization was commissioned by BBC Radio 4 and broadcast over a weekend in late summer, 2004. Much of Homer's *Odyssey* is written as narrated poem, and when characters do enter into discourse, it tends to be with formal speech, rather than what we might call dialogue. Faced with that situation, the role of the dramatist is to transform such narration into a series of conversations and exchanges, and to actualize some of its unspoken intentions by putting speech into characters' mouths. In other words, to get people to talk. It would be impossible, not to mention pointless, to perform such a transformation without running a few risks and taking a few liberties. And yet the version presented here hopes never to stray *too* far from the content, chronology and atmosphere of the original. It is not set in a housing estate in Salford. It does not depict the Achaeans as veterans of the Gulf War or asylum-seekers, though of course we should not be surprised if the *Odyssey* rings with echoes and resonances of our contemporary world. Such is the power and purpose of myth.

My thanks are due to Janet Whittaker for conceiving and directing this project, and for having the honesty to tell me that two other authors initially associated with the commission subsequently passed away. Tackling these colossal old texts is a huge and daunting undertaking. On delivery of the final manuscript, I wrote on the final page, 'Can I die now?' Many thanks also to Peter Jones for his advice and comments. Finally, I owe a huge debt of gratitude to those ranks of scholars and authors, some of whom spent a lifetime translating the *Odyssey* from a twelve-thousand-line, two-and-a-half-thousand-year-old epic into the contemporary literature of their day. Of the modern translations, those by E. V. Rieu, Richmond Lattimore and Robert Fagles have inspired and illuminated the most.

One more thing. Although this version of the *Odyssey* was developed as a radio play and is presented here in script form, it was always in the back of my mind that it should have a further life as a piece of writing. Not just something to be performed, but something to read. A book, in fact.

Simon Armitage

Remind us, Muse, of that man of many means,
sent spinning the length and breadth of the map
after bringing the towers of Troy to their knees;

of the lessons he learned in the cities of great minds,
and the heartbreak he suffered, roaming the seas
to land his shipmates and salvage his life.

But for all the torture and grief he sustained
his comrades were lost; heedless fools,
they gorged on the flesh of the Cattle of the Sun.
In turn, the God of the Sun made death their domain.

Muse, daughter of Memory and Zeus,
where to start this story is yours to choose.

I

OLYMPUS

*A council of the Gods. A dozen or so voices are chattering
amongst themselves.*

ZEUS

What I say is this:
Odysseus must be punished.
Poseidon must have his revenge.

General agreement amongst the Gods.

ATHENA

But why, father? This man was a hero at Troy.
One of our favourites.

ZEUS

We owe him no special favour.
He's a human in the end. A mortal.

ATHENA

There's no shame in being human.

ZEUS

They stumble from one tragedy to the next,
never improving, never learning from their mistakes,
then blame us for their frailties and faults.
Their misfortunes are their own!
Our words of warning fall on deaf ears
and they turn a blind eye to our signs.
When we send eagles
to signal our thoughts in the sky,
what do they do – stand and point and stare,
like . . . birdwatchers!

After all these years you'd expect some change,
some progress, some development – some sense.
But their behaviour gets worse.
They are children, squabbling brats,
and the world is their kindergarten.

ATHENA

There are always exceptions to the rule, aren't there,
   father?

ZEUS

And exceptions that prove it as well.

ATHENA

All I'm saying is . . . we shouldn't be so quick to judge.
Take each case on its merits. See the person,
not just the species as a whole. Consider the man.

ZEUS

Consider Odysseus – that's what you mean, isn't it?
Speak up, child.

ATHENA

Well, yes, he's an example of the kind of thing I'm talking
   about.

Groans from the other Gods.

ATHENA (*stridently*)

His predicament is a shadow on my heart
and grows darker every day.

It's only yesterday you Gods were cheering him on.
Praising his cunning and skill, toasting the way
he conjured victory out of defeat at Troy,
imagined a hollow horse made from a ship's beams.

HERMES

His savages butchered and ate the Cattle of the Sun – those beautiful, lumbering bulls that never hurt anyone.

ATHENA

That's rich coming from you.
You – the world's first cattle rustler.
Fifty heifers, wasn't it, stolen from Apollo?

HERMES

I was an infant. It was a prank.
I gave forty-eight of them back.

ATHENA

I thought you of all people would be more sympathetic.
You – the God of Travellers, the Light in the Dark.

HERMES

I helped him once. I pointed out the moly flower,
saved him from being magicked into a hog.

ATHENA

That was years ago. He's still lost.

HERMES

Is it my job to hold his hand all the way home?

ATHENA

Do you have some more important task?

HERMES

Well, I . . .

ATHENA

Don't expect fires to be lit or bulls to be slaughtered
in your name, if the prayers of a struggling traveller
fall on deaf ears. Don't expect temples and grottoes.

HERMES
My image appears by every path,
in every roadside shrine.

ATHENA
Roads and paths alter their course. Humans have fickle
hearts.

HERMES
It isn't a popularity contest.

ATHENA
You'll be forgotten. Wiped from memory.

HERMES
Ridiculous.

ATHENA
You won't exist.

HERMES (*after a few moments of thought*)
I suppose a little nudge in the right direction wouldn't
hurt.

ZEUS
Odysseus blinded the Cyclops. Seared his only eye with a
burning branch.
The Cyclops. Poseidon's son. My nephew no less!

ATHENA
Put yourself in Odysseus' shoes and tell me how it feels.
Twenty years away from his land . . .

ANOTHER GOD (*pipes up*)
Nineteen.

ATHENA
Ten years fighting and winning the war at Troy,

[8]

ten more making his journey home,
seven of those snared in Calypso's net.
Calypso, who charms him with voodoo words,
encircles him with her legs,
blows mumbo-jumbo into his ears to make him forget.
But he doesn't forget.
He dreams of the fires of Ithaca,
scans the horizon for smoke,
weeps for his people, his wife and his son.
And after all the sacrifices he made in your name, father.
I don't know how you sleep.

ZEUS

Yes, true, he's suffered more than most, but . . .

ATHENA

And his tired wife, Penelope, who waits.

ZEUS

Penelope, yes, she's patient to the last.

ATHENA

And Telemachus, his son. A young man now
who was only a babe in arms when his father's boat
sailed out of the bay.

ZEUS

True. A crying shame.

ATHENA

And the loyal people of his home town . . .

ZEUS

All right. ALL RIGHT!
No one forgets proud Odysseus,
stuck there on some forsaken rock in Calypso's web.

But my brother Poseidon harbours a deep grudge.
He wants blood.

ATHENA (*with obvious flattery*)
Father. Father . . . most noble Zeus . . .

ZEUS
On the other hand, no one would deny the man a fighting
chance.

The Gods mumble and grumble amongst themselves.

ZEUS (*whispering*)
Well, Athena. Here's your moment. What do you suggest?

ATHENA (*struggling to make herself heard*)
Dispatch Hermes to that bewitching nymph,
tell her to untangle Odysseus from her spell.
Let him sail home under a stiff breeze.

ZEUS (*angry*)
You'll do me the honour of listening to Zeus' daughter.

Silence in the hall.

Hermes, fly off to that bewitching nymph,
tell her to untangle Odysseus from her spell.
Let him sail home under a stiff breeze.
He can take his chances on the high sea.

All the Gods shall unite and agree.

Murmurings of dissent from the Gods.

(*with great thunder*)
ZEUS HAS SPOKEN. ALL THE GODS SHALL AGREE.

Silence. Then the Gods disperse. In agreement.

ATHENA

> My father, mightiest of the mighty,
> highest among the high . . .

ZEUS

> That's enough worming and wheedling for one day.
> And what part shall you play in all this?

ATHENA

> I'll go to Ithaca with a plan.
> Light a fire in the mind of Telemachus, Odysseus' only
> son,
> put fuel in his thoughts.

ZEUS

> Why such haste?
> After twenty years, is there any need to rush?

ATHENA

> For us immortals, time is a circle that never ends.
> But man has a fistful of sand and treasures every grain.

ZEUS

> You are your father's daughter, no doubt of that.

ATHENA

> I'll take this spear. Disguise myself as Mentes,
> an old friend of Odysseus.
> I'll appear as a man – in the flesh.

ITHACA. THE PALACE OF ODYSSEUS.

The suitors are drinking, feasting and playing games. They throw dice, arm-wrestle and occasionally break out into bawdy songs.

ANTINOUS
More wine over here.

EURYMACHUS
And the good stuff from the far cellar, mind.
Not the piss you keep for unwanted guests.
And more pig.
Succulent suckling pig with its crackling skin.

AMPHINOMUS
Steady on a bit. There's no need to go over the top.

ANTINOUS
Let him talk.

EURYMACHUS
And its tender roll of loin . . .
And its supple flanks . . .

And its virgin balls . . .

ANTINOUS
Speaking of which, here comes our host.
(*to Telemachus*)
Telemachus, a delicious feast again.
Your kitchen does you proud.

TELEMACHUS
Never let it be said that you starved.

[12]

EURYMACHUS

And the wine – quite delicious.
Zeus himself would smile at the taste.

TELEMACHUS

If there's any left when you're finished
I'll be glad to offer him a glass.

You'll have to excuse me, though.
A visitor stands in the door,
another stranger I'll make welcome in my father's house.

ANTINOUS

Be my guest.

*The suitors laugh behind his back as Telemachus walks
away.*

TELEMACHUS (*wearily*)

One more mouth to feed. Well, don't stand in the porch.

MENTES (*Athena in disguise*)

Not the most heartfelt welcome I've ever had.

TELEMACHUS

We never turn our back on visitors,
but you suitors are eating us out of house and home.
Don't expect to be welcomed with open arms.

MENTES

I'm no suitor.
I'm Mentes, a friend of your father's from a long way
    back.

TELEMACHUS (*eagerly*)

You have news of my father? Where is he?
Has he sent you ahead to announce his arrival?

MENTES

    No news like that I'm afraid.

TELEMACHUS

    Then what brings you to Ithaca?

MENTES

    I'm . . . anchored in the bay with my men,
    en route to Temese to trade metal and ore.
    I stopped in to pay my respects.

Bawdy singing rises in the background.

MENTES

    Forgive me, but this is a scandal.
    What gives those men the right to behave like swine
    in the house of noble Odysseus?

TELEMACHUS

    Let's step outside for some fresh air as we talk.

They go outside.

    Two decades ago my father sailed out of view
    and we haven't set eyes on him since.
    For years and years I imagined him standing
    where you stood just moments ago,
    filling the frame of the door,
    back to throw his arms around his family
    and claim his house.
    But now I fear the worst.

MENTES

    A man like Odysseus wouldn't just disappear without
      trace.

TELEMACHUS

I have a nightmare vision when I close my eyes.
My father, dead and alone on some stony plain,
or deep in an ocean trench. He's water now, or he's dust.

MENTES

You sound like you've given up hope.

TELEMACHUS

And there's more pain to bear:
these men that lounge on his rugs
and loaf at his hearth,
grazing and gulping their way through our wealth,
these 'suitors' lay claim to my mother's heart.
But because my father has no tomb or grave
she can't say no and she can't say yes.
So they gorge themselves at our expense
and we feed them on silver plates.
We're besieged, from inside our own house!

MENTES

Telemachus, listen to me. I'm no teller of fortunes
and I can't read the meaning of birds in the sky.
But the Gods have put a thought in my mind;
for your own sake you should act on what I say.

I believe these suitors will shriek for forgiveness before
    they die.

TELEMACHUS

It's a mouth-watering thought. If I were more of a
    man . . .

MENTES

Get a boat of twenty oars.
Sail to Pylos then Sparta,

seek news of your father from his friends.
They'll tell you of the glorious victory at Troy.
They'll inspire you. You'll grow with every word.

TELEMACHUS
No, they'll meet me on the pier, awkward in grief,
like distant uncles consoling a dead man's son,
saying how sorry they were to hear of my loss.
Then I'll be crushed.

MENTES
If you hear of his death
then heap stones on a plot of earth
and call it his grave.
Then your mother Penelope must choose her groom.

But if you hear word that he lives,
sail back to Ithaca, and hold yourself proud and straight.

TELEMACHUS
You speak with a fatherly tone.

MENTES
You're no longer a child, Telemachus.
It's time to prove that to yourself.
Now go back inside. I'll make myself scarce.

TELEMACHUS
Wait . . .

Athena leaves.

My father had friends in high places,
friends of unusual nature, other-worldly . . .

*The voices of the suitors rise again. Over them comes the
voice of a minstrel, Phemios.*

PHEMIOS (*sings*)

How many boats for Helen of Troy?
How many boats, how many boats,
How many trees were cut to their knees
to bring her back over the ocean?

How many weapons for Helen of Troy?
How many arrows, how many spears,
how many sorrows and how many tears
to bring her back over the ocean?

How many miles for Helen of Troy?
How many miles, how many miles,
how many days in the wild of the waves
to bring her back over the ocean?

How many soldiers for Helen of Troy?
How much force and how much blood,
how many foals from a horse made of wood
to bring her back over the ocean?

How many lives for Helen of Troy?
How many lives, how many lives,
how many husbands and how many wives
to bring her back over the ocean?

Penelope appears at the head of the stairs. The room falls
silent. The minstrel's song grinds to a halt.

ANTINOUS

Penelope. You grace us with your presence.

EURYMACHUS

You honour us.

AMPHINOMUS

Here's a seat by the fire, and a cloak for your shoulders.

PENELOPE
    It was music that stirred me.

PHEMIOS
    Thank you, my lady.

PENELOPE
    Troubled me, I mean.
    Roused me out of the comfort of sleep.
    Have you only the one song?

PHEMIOS
    No, lady. Thousands.

PENELOPE
    Then sing another. Not the song of Troy.
    It climbed my stairs, rising like smoke,
    seeping under the door and bringing me to tears.
    Let me sleep. I'm tired.

Penelope retires. The suitors mutter amongst themselves.

EURYMACHUS
    She's an icy one.

ANTINOUS
    She'll melt.

EURYMACHUS
    I know what I'd be like after twenty years with my legs
        crossed.
    I'd be at boiling point.

AMPHINOMUS
    Beautiful, though. Standing there at the head of the stairs.
    Against the evening light.

EURYMACHUS

She takes her wedding vows too seriously.
She takes her fidelity too far.

AMPHINOMUS

That's why we want her, isn't it?
That's why we're queuing up for her hand.
We want that faithfulness for ourselves.

EURYMACHUS

And everything that comes with it.

ANTINOUS

Property.

EURYMACHUS

Weaponry.

ANTINOUS

Lakes of wine.

EURYMACHUS

Herds of cattle.

ANTINOUS

Gold.

EURYMACHUS

Fame.

AMPHINOMUS

My intentions are entirely honourable.

EURYMACHUS

So are mine. It's just that I've got some very big
intentions!

ANTINOUS

It's like a land of plenty waiting behind a locked gate.
One day she'll say yes, and give one man amongst us the
    key.
The key to paradise.
When she stood there just now,
with the sun behind her, illuminated, the last rays of dusk
making a filament of her body beneath her dress,
which of us didn't steal a glimpse of what lies ahead, on
    the other side . . .

TELEMACHUS (*furiously*)

You suitors, camped out at our expense,
gnawing your way like rats through our estate,
I'll keep you fed and watered
for as long as you stay – it's what society expects.
But if there were justice in this world,
Zeus would punish you for your gluttony,
he'd put an end to your infinite appetites,
and I for one would give him endless thanks.

EURYMACHUS (*aside*)

What's that bed-wetter whining about now?

ANTINOUS

Telemachus, what's got into you?
How dare you talk with such impertinence,
as if the Gods had given you leave to speak?

TELEMACHUS

For as long as my father Odysseus is away
I'll be lord and master in this house,
I'll be the owner of all his hard-won fortunes
and I'll speak as I please.

EURYMACHUS
Say what you will,
the outcome of all this lies in the lap of the Gods,
and there's nothing you can do to alter what they decide.

ANTINOUS
Correct.
Anyway, who was the visitor who arrived unannounced,
then vanished into thin air?
Another suitor, joining the long and winding queue,
or just a tinker pushing some second-rate goods?

TELEMACHUS
A friend of my father's – a merchant trading shore to shore.
He stopped to pay his respects
but when he set his eyes on this vulgar scene
he made his excuses and ran to catch the wind.

ANTINOUS
That tone of voice again, Telemachus.
Well, let me say this, if we have become debased
there's only your mother to blame.
There's a name for people like her.
We could have been off in the wide world,
lying beside any woman who took our fancy –
but good Penelope keeps us hanging on.
For nearly four years we've dangled on a string
while she sends us encouraging nods and winks.
We've invested too much time to just walk away.

TELEMACHUS
She is a faithful mother and wife.

ANTINOUS
She's a clever trickster as well. What was it she said to us?

'All you who flatter me
and are eager for my hand,
let me first weave this shroud
for Laertes my father-in-law,
who is frail and old.'

EURYMACHUS
    'What will the womenfolk think of me
    if he dies without a sheet
    to wind his royal body in?'

ANTINOUS
    'When the weaving's done,
    when the shroud's complete,
    then I'll choose a man.'

So we let her weave.
Season after season, year after year we let her weave,
until one of her maids whispered in my ear
that what she stitched by day she unpicked at night.
That's the kind of devious mind we're up against.

TELEMACHUS
    She plays for time, holding out hope for my father's
        return.
    Who could blame her for that?

EURYMACHUS
    She's a vixen. Cunning and sly.

AMPHINOMUS
    Telemachus, your mother is a prize worthy of any
        man . . .

ANTINOUS
    Burn this into your brain, Telemachus:

we'll not give up the chase,
so the quicker you cut the apron strings
and marry her off to whichever suitor she most deserves,
the better for everyone concerned.

The door bursts open. Halitherses staggers in, breathless.

HALITHERSES
A sign in the sky.

EURYMACHUS
Who's this old bag of bones?

TELEMACHUS
Halitherses. He has a knack for reading the flight of birds.
Tell us what you saw.

HALITHERSES
Two eagles soaring over the town.

ANTINOUS
It happens every day.

HALITHERSES
They glided side by side,
then suddenly turned on each other in mid-air,
lashing out with their fearful talons,
tearing feathers with their terrible beaks, making an
    ungodly din . . .
It spells disaster for you suitors.
It means bloody misfortune is being plotted somewhere
    overhead . . .

EURYMACHUS
That's crap.
Someone take this coffin-dodger outside and leave him
    to rot.

HALITHERSES
It's not crap. There'll be ructions.

EURYMACHUS
You couldn't predict your way out of your own hat!
Save your breath, incontinent old corpse.
And here's a forecast for you: if you can find your way
    home,
tell your children what fate has in store for them
if their father keeps opening his trap.

HALITHERSES
I'm not wrong. You'll see that I'm not.

AMPHINOMUS
I know something about this kind of thing.
He's right when he says that two eagles mean trouble.

ANTINOUS
Birds do peculiar things every day of the week.
They're just birds. It's . . . ornithology.

HALITHERSES (*rather pathetically*)
I've predicted all kinds of things. I'm good at it.

ANTINOUS
You're a shit-stirrer, that's what you are.
Odysseus is as dead as stone and everyone knows it.
So why put ideas of vengeance in his son's head?
Telemachus should be left to finish his grieving,
then his mother could be married off.

TELEMACHUS
I have a proposition for you men.

EURYMACHUS
You're hardly in a position to bargain . . .

ANTINOUS

Let him speak.

TELEMACHUS

Allow me a ship and twenty men to row.
I'll sail to Pylos, then on to Sparta,
and ask for hard news of my father,
find the man who last saw him alive
or the man who pronounced him dead.
If he lives, grant me another year,
twelve months for him to find Ithaca.
If he has perished, I'll build a tomb
in his name, and make offerings
in his honour, in keeping with his fame.
Then one man here shall marry his widow.

EURYMACHUS (*hushed, under the hubbub of voices*)

It's a trick. He's plotting our murder.

AMPHINOUS

It seems a reasonable enough request.

EURYMACHUS

He'll bring back an army
or recipes for poison to mix with our supper.
He's as slippery as his mother.

ANTINOUS

Maybe.
But he's young, inexperienced and full of idiot ideas.
More likely he'll drown at sea.
Which will make our job here a whole lot smoother.
Whoever marries the mother could keep the house –
the family's worldly goods we'll split between us.
There's nothing to lose. He's played right into our hands.

(to Telemachus)
Very well.
Bon voyage, Telemachus:
we'll scan the waves for your safe return.

ON ITHACA'S BEACH AT NIGHT

Telemachus is alone.

TELEMACHUS
You who came to me in my father's house,
a Goddess in the body of a man, who set my pulse racing
with a plan, can you hear me now?

ATHENA (*appearing out of the air*)
Your journey waits for you, Telemachus.
It's a test of your mind and your strength,
and a test of your birth: prove to yourself
that you are your father's son, that his blood
is in your blood, and you'll journey into joy.
Pull yourself up to your full height.
You have a lot to live up to. Many sons
are blocked out by their father's light;
the bigger and stronger the parent tree,
the weaker the stripling, standing in its shade.
But I think you'll grow tall and straight.
Here's a fast ship, fitted out, ready to sail.
Collect provisions for the trip – stuff satchels
with meal and top up the jars with strong wine.

TELEMACHUS
The suitors seemed suspicious.
If I return to the house they might . . .

ATHENA
They're too busy roasting meat and swilling drink
to bother with you. Don't lose confidence now.
Screw your courage to a point. For my part,

I'll steal through the town recruiting the best men.
They won't say no when they see into my eyes.

Start plotting a course, Telemachus, the stars
point the way tonight, under clear, open skies.

PENELOPE'S BED-CHAMBER

Penelope half-sings, half-hums the final verse of Phemios'
Song of Troy.

EURYCLEIA
  Come back from the window, my lady. There's a chill
    wind tonight.

PENELOPE
  My son stands on the beach.

EURYCLEIA
  Looking for signs of his father. Hopeful to the last.

PENELOPE
  Two sets of footprints on the sand,
  but he stands alone.

EURYCLEIA
  He'll be pacing up and down. That's what I do when I'm
    nervous.

PENELOPE
  And the wind blows the wrong way
  for this time of night, away from the shore.

EURYCLEIA
  It's a chill wind all right. Straight off the mountains.
  Come away from the window now and take this cloak.

PENELOPE
  Do you hear what those young men say about me?

EURYCLEIA
  Take no notice.

PENELOPE

That I'm carved from ice.

EURYCLEIA

From standing at that window in a chill wind.

PENELOPE

That I give them knowing looks, feed them with hope.

EURYCLEIA

What do they know about a woman's face?

PENELOPE

That I'm the one making the situation worse.

EURYCLEIA

It's the drink in them that talks. They're loud-mouths, and louder still with a jar of wine in their gut.

PENELOPE

It's true, though, isn't it?

EURYCLEIA

What's true?

PENELOPE

That I'm the corn that keeps the locusts fed.

EURYCLEIA

Don't torture yourself.

PENELOPE

But I'm right, aren't I?

EURYCLEIA

I'm a brusher of hair and a hanger of clothes – I'm not paid for my wit.

PENELOPE

Yes, it's unfair of me . . .

EURYCLEIA

But since you're asking, I'll tell you how it is.
You live like a widow, with no man at your side,
and you've lived like that for nigh on twenty years.
Until you bury Odysseus, you're still his wife.
It pays to be cold on the outside
with that lot down there drooling at your feet
and sniffing under the bedroom door.
But I know you. I've known you for donkey's years,
and there's a flame somewhere inside, right?
In your heart, I shouldn't wonder, and it won't go out.

PENELOPE

Shouldn't I snuff it dead, for everyone's sake?

EURYCLEIA

No one can change what's in their own heart.
Not even a queen. And that's as much as I know on the
    topic.

PENELOPE

Maybe he's found a better pillow for his head,
next to a younger woman with silkier flesh.

EURYCLEIA

She'd have to be made from silk itself to have skin any
    silkier than yours.
I've known some skin in my time and yours is the silkiest
    of the lot.
There's skin and there's skin, and let me tell you, yours is
    pure silk.

PENELOPE

> You underestimate your powers of argument.
> You should sit in the council of the wise.

EURYCLEIA

> Why, do they need a brusher of hair?
> Now, don't be going to that window again, it's a chill
>   wind
> from the mountain. You'll get a ghost in your lungs.
> And if that's everything I'll say goodnight.

Eurycleia leaves.

PENELOPE

> Would that be so bad?
> To end it, inhale a cold death?

She breathes deeply.

> To join my husband on the other side,
> is that what the Gods have in mind?

OLYMPUS

ZEUS

Athena, my daughter, give me a progress report.
You were a visitation in Ithaca overnight.
Are the vultures still circling the house of Odysseus?

ATHENA

They are.

ZEUS

And what of his son, young Telemachus?
Has he formulated a plan?
Has he 'hatched from the egg of his inaction?'

ATHENA

He has.

ZEUS

And is patient Penelope still faithfulness itself?

ATHENA

She is.

ZEUS

I hope you were discreet. It doesn't do to meddle too
    much.
Makes them dependent.
Makes them over-reliant upon our interventions.

ATHENA

I was subtle and tactful. I've blown a gentle breeze
into the sails of the situation – it's what was called for.
But things need a further push. Odysseus
was like a father to his people, almost Godlike;

now it's shameful to hear his friends and neighbours
speak so casually of him. His name slips from memory.
He's like a great ship that sank on its return journey,
lost and only half-remembered, under the surface.

ZEUS

At least they don't live for ever, like us. My memory –
it's like a museum. Infinite rooms, covered in dust.

ATHENA

We need to be active on all fronts.
My brother, Hermes, when will he . . .

ZEUS

Already flown. Just after dawn he collected his spear,
pulled his laces tight, and putting his best foot first
went island-hopping over the waves to Calypso's cave.
She's a crafty one, though. She won't give up her catch
just like that. Let's hope our messenger keeps his nerve.

ATHENA

She has a soft spot for Hermes. He'll talk her round.

ZEUS

She has a soft spot for Odysseus too, we might say!
And a double-jointed tongue.

Here, I'll blow a hole in the clouds. Let's watch.

CALYPSO'S ISLAND

Hermes approaches the mouth of the cave. Inside, Calypso is singing quietly to herself.

CALYPSO (*sings*)
  Fountains like pillars of light
  light these meadows
  of wild-grown flowers and wild herbs
  on the path to her cave.

  The limbs of the cedar
  alight in the hearth.
  Sweet-smoking cedar breathes incense
  out of the cave's mouth.

  Vines clustered with grapes.
  Leaves of the alder, sprigs of the poplar
  and cypress cones litter the floor
  of the cave's mouth.

  Land-birds nest in the beard
  of grasses and ferns
  at the cave's mouth.
  Overhead, seabirds mew and meep,

  wheeling up and wheeling down,
  riding the thermals, riding the warmth
  from the cave's mouth.

HERMES (*taking up the song*)
  And down in the cave itself,

  out of the cave's throat,
  a woman's song. A woman's voice,

fine, carried light as a thread of hair
floating on thin air.

CALYPSO

What do you want?

HERMES

Calypso, I've travelled over vast, empty plains
of the sea and there's salt on my tongue.
Before we speak, won't you offer an old friend a drink?

CALYPSO

It's true there's a common bond between us, Hermes.
I'd go further than that even – I'm fond of you.
But no one travels to this far-flung outcrop
just to marvel at the violets in the fields
or drink the fresh water – pure as it is.

HERMES

Come into the light – let me see your face.

CALYPSO

I'll help if I can, but I suspect the worst.

HERMES

You're being straightforward with me,
I respect you for that, and I'll be honest in return.
I speak to you as one God to another;
you might have chosen to live like a mortal,
earth-bound and modest, but a God is what you are.
So you know that when word comes from Olympus
it can't be ignored, and when those words
come from the mouth of Zeus himself, they're arrows of
    iron
which won't be deflected or stopped.

CALYPSO

And he fires his iron words in my direction, does he?
I can guess why.

HERMES

He says at night you sleep next to a man.
No crime in itself, except that man is Odysseus,
who fought and won the long battle for Troy
and was shipwrecked here on his voyage home.
He's been a prisoner in your keep for seven years now,
and I'm instructed to instruct you to let him go.

CALYPSO

He's no prisoner. He can leave when he likes.

HERMES

And what would he sail in, a walnut shell?

CALYPSO

He loves me! Why would he want to risk his neck?

HERMES

Well, let's ask him, shall we? Where is he now?

CALYPSO

On his favourite rock overlooking the bay.

HERMES

Looking east towards Ithaca, no doubt.

CALYPSO

He's happy. He's never tried to escape.

HERMES

That rock he sits on was visible from miles out at sea.
Bleached white, and not by the dung of birds
or the throw of the sea, but by a man's tears.

CALYPSO (*angry*)

You Gods on your mountain perch, you're a joke.
You're the high-priests of hypocrisy.
When a male God swoops down on a woman
or forces himself on some innocent young thing,
you call it Fate. When a female God
falls for a mortal or takes a man into her bed
an earthquake of disapproval blows its top.

HERMES

You're confusing politics with matters of the heart.
He loves his wife, Penelope. He wasn't yours to
take.

CALYPSO

Not mine? Not mine? That's the richest yet.
Who found him clinging to the keel of his boat
at the height of the storm? Who plucked him
out of the thrashing waves, kissed breath
back into his lungs, pumped his heart with blood,
nursed him back to strength, rolled him in love?
Not mine? Without me there is no Odysseus.

HERMES

You saved him from death. Does that mean he owes
you his life?

CALYPSO

I saved him from Poseidon, who clicked his fingers
and smashed his boat to splinters
and turned the ocean bed into a mass grave.
While Zeus looked the other way, no doubt.

HERMES

You should speak more quietly.

This cave amplifies an angry voice,
throws sounds upwards into the skies.

CALYPSO

Let it ring loud in the spirals of Zeus' ear.
If it's decided, what difference can it make?

HERMES

You can't win –
why make it more difficult for yourself?
Besides which, his actions aren't yours to judge.
Be glad you don't carry the burden of the world.

Don't light a fuse under the temper of mighty Zeus.

CALYPSO

This is a water-locked land, with no ships at anchor.

HERMES

You'll think of something. Use your ingenuity.

CALYPSO

Do you think I can just whistle and the navy appears?

HERMES

You saved him once, you can save him again.

CALYPSO

Well, if he drowns, don't lay the blame at my feet.
I don't want disfiguring with a thunderbolt.

HERMES

If you care for Odysseus as you say you do
you'll see him safe and sound out of the bay.
And if he's as keen to see his homeland as I think he is,
he'll take care of himself after that.

Will you give Odysseus the news, or shall I?

CALYPSO

You fly off home, errand boy.
I'll say my own goodbye.

ODYSSEUS ON THE ROCK

Calypso finds Odysseus looking out to sea. He is weeping.

CALYPSO

Tearful Odysseus. You could have been my God.

ODYSSEUS

Tears are human. They make me a man.

CALYPSO

You've wept an ocean from those eyes.

ODYSSEUS

If I had, I'd plunge into it here and now
and swim for home, buoyed up by the salt.
But this island sucks up everything I am.

CALYPSO

I am to give you up, Odysseus.

ODYSSEUS

You've tormented me too long for your jibes to hurt.

CALYPSO

But have I ever told you lies? Look into my face.

ODYSSEUS

It's a trick.

CALYPSO

Look into my eyes. Listen to my voice.
You're free to leave. I'm to give you up.

ODYSSEUS

Give me up? Give me up to what? Feed me to the sharks,
do you mean?

Put me to sea on a log so the waves can snap my bones?
Is that how you spit me out
after chewing the best years out of my life?

CALYPSO

The sharks aren't my pets. I don't control the waves.
But I'll help you leave by whatever means I possess.

ODYSSEUS

Why? I need to know why.

CALYPSO

Be happy to be heading home and don't ask.
Fate has decided, and no one can contradict fate.

ODYSSEUS

Fate lies in the flick of your wrist. You're a Goddess.

CALYPSO

Then don't dare interrogate me – treat me with respect.
Think of it, a Goddess indeed, who offered herself
to a mere man. But that man pines for his earthly wife.
By day you weep. At night, I pull you onto my body
and you only half-resist, but your thoughts are elsewhere
and you close your eyes to see Penelope's face.
So ask me nothing else. I might not have the human touch
you seem to crave, Odysseus, but I have my pride.
You should be grateful before I change my mind.

ODYSSEUS

It's true then? I'm free to go?
(*flattering her, not wanting to lose his chance*)
Calypso, have I ever once compared you to her?
My wife's face fades in my memory each day,
and that's what I can't bear. That's why I ache.
But your beauty will never dim because you never age.

CALYPSO

Your tongue was always your sharpest weapon.

ODYSSEUS

But it never cut you, no matter how close you came.

CALYPSO

Take this axe. Choose the sturdiest trees
for a raft, and build a hold on the deck.
I'll stow it with water and food
and wine to ease the passing of days.
I'll stitch warm clothes onto your back
and hang a full white sail from the mast.

ODYSSEUS

Can all this be true? Are the Gods smiling on me at last?

CALYPSO

I'm giving you my word. Here, give me your hand.

Lie with me one more night and leave at dawn.
Feel for yourself the compassionate heart in my breast.

THE PALACE OF ODYSSEUS

The suitors are dining.

EURYMACHUS
Bring me some horse.

AMPHINOMUS
You're drunk. We don't eat horse. Do we?

EURYMACHUS
I'll eat anything when I'm hungry.

ANTINOUS
You'll eat anything even when you're not.

EURYMACHUS
The stomach expects it.
Have you ever seen the inside of a man?

AMPHINOMUS
In battle, there was a wounded . . .

EURYMACHUS
I once tied a dead man's gut to a post
and fastened the other end to a messenger boy
and sent him off.
He walked for more than a mile and it still didn't snap.
It's elastic!
There's no limit to what you can trough,
and once you've stretched your appetite like that,
it's no good just eating a light snack.
Your stomach demands more.
(*shouts*)
Bring me some horse!

ANTINOUS

We should have tied such a gut
to Odysseus' son. Kept a hold on him.

EURYMACHUS

It was your idea to let him go.

ANTINOUS

So it was. But now I'm troubled by second thoughts.

AMPHINOMUS

You said he was only a boy. You said he'd drown.

ANTINOUS

I did.
Then I heard he'd taken the swiftest boat
in the land, and a careful choice of supplies,
and hand-picked the best crew in town.
And something else.

EURYMACHUS

What?

ANTINOUS

He was seen on the beach that night, in deep talk
with that shady visitor – remember the one?

AMPHINOMUS

The friend of his father's?
Who disappeared as mysteriously as he came?

ANTINOUS

That's what I was told.

AMPHINOMUS

Maybe the old man was right, about those eagles
grappling in mid-air. I found a feather
in the courtyard that night, right under my foot . . .

EURYMACHUS
 So what? I found a beetle in my shoe. So what?

ANTINOUS
 Exactly. So what? On the other hand . . .

AMPHINOMUS
 On the other hand . . .?

ANTINOUS
 We should put to sea.

AMPHINOMUS
 He'll be out of reach by now.
 We'll never catch him up.

ANTINOUS
 Not catch him up. More subtle than that.
 We should lie in wait.

EURYMACHUS
 I like the sound of this. Go on.

ANTINOUS
 On his return leg,
 Telemachus will sail that strait of water
 between the cliffs of Samos and Ithaca's coast.
 He might be planning a surprise for us,
 but we'll have a bigger surprise for him.

EURYMACHUS
 Yes, yes.

ANTINOUS
 We'll flag him down, like a welcome party
 meaning to sail with him into his home port.

[46]

EURYMACHUS
    That's crafty. Very crafty.

ANTINOUS
    We'll come alongside . . . and the rest
    we can leave to our imaginations, for now.
    Except to say
    he won't put so much as his little toe on home soil again.
        Agreed?

EURYMACHUS
    Agreed.

AMPHINOMUS
    You're talking about murder. Murdering the son
    of the woman you hope to marry.

ANTINOUS
    She'll marry no one if he comes sailing home from sunny
        Pylos
    bronzed with his father's reputation, swaggering and
        walking tall.
    Besides, she'll think he drowned by accident.
    Then she'll need a shoulder to cry on.

    But keep it under your tongues,
    we don't want loose talk whispering through the vaults
    or echoing into the upstairs chambers.

Their mumbling voices carry into the corridors of the house.

PENELOPE'S BED-CHAMBER

There is a tap at the door.

EURYCLEIA
　My lady?

PENELOPE
　Eurycleia?

EURYCLEIA
　Yes. Me, my lady.

PENELOPE
　I didn't call for you. It's too early.

Eurycleia taps at the door again.

EURYCLEIA
　My lady. My lady.

PENELOPE (*to herself*)
　Time has stuck its fingers
　in the old nurse's ears.
　I said you're excused.
　At least don't stand pawing at the door like a stray dog.
　Haven't we known each other long enough to . . .
　(*She opens the door.*)
　Eurycleia?

EURYCLEIA
　My lady. Forgive me.

PENELOPE
　Forgive you for what?
　Are the suitors skriking for more food?

[48]

Are they screaming like baby birds,
can't we feed them quick enough?
Well, open the doors of the granary
and the vaults where the meats are kept cold.
Let them gorge till they burst.

EURYCLEIA

If only they'd stuffed themselves silly,
then maybe I wouldn't be standing here like this.

PENELOPE

Standing like what?

EURYCLEIA

Like the thing that I am.
A raggedy old woman with bad news.

PENELOPE

What bad news?

EURYCLEIA

Don't hate me for it . . .

PENELOPE

Spit it out.

EURYCLEIA

It's Telemachus. He's gone.

PENELOPE

Gone where?

EURYCLEIA

Sailed off in search of his father. He was overheard on the
    beach, making plans. And seen at the front of a ship as
    it left the bay.

PENELOPE
  Without telling me? Without saying . . .

EURYCLEIA
  And there's worse, my lady. Oh, don't be hating me for
    this.

PENELOPE
  Say all of it. Tell it in one piece.

EURYCLEIA
  Those slavering letches downstairs. Those drooling
    mongrels not fit to kiss the soles of your shoes. They're
    planning . . .

PENELOPE
  All of it.

EURYCLEIA
  . . . planning his death.
  They'll lie in wait between the rocks. Cut him off on his
    way back. Meet his body with bronze spears. They say
    he'll never set foot on his homeland again. Oh my
    lady . . .

PENELOPE
  So either way he's lost. Sucked down by the sea
  on his journey out, or slaughtered by cowards
  within touching distance of his own shore, in front of his
    mother's eyes.
  First my husband was blown out of reach.
  Now the wind carries my son off like a weightless seed.

  Why wasn't I told?

EURYCLEIA
  We were feared. There was only me daft enough.

Only me with a tongue that wasn't tied.
And anyway, he made me swear an oath.

PENELOPE

What oath?

EURYCLEIA

To say nothing – that's what I had to swear. So I was
torn down the middle, either to his loyalty, or to
yours. And he looked at me with a face like metal and
made me swear. Didn't want your beautiful skin
staining with tears – that's what he said. But if I did
wrong, then have me killed, my lady, and I'll not
complain. If I made the wrong choice, I'll hang up this
life on its peg. Like an old coat. Then you'll not be
nuisanced by me again.

PENELOPE

You were given no choice.
There will be no more talk of death.

EURYCLEIA

My lady.

PENELOPE

No more talk of loss.
(*She sways.*)
See how heavy my heart has swollen,
it pitches within me and bundles me over.
Steady me with your hand.

EURYCLEIA (*relieved, and full of love*)

Here's my hand, my lady, and your lovely hand in it.
Take strong hold of me. Let's wash with water, and I'll
find fresh clothes from the laundry. We'll go to the
upper house and pray to Athena.

PENELOPE (*tearful*)
My only son.

EURYCLEIA
And Odysseus' son – there'll be Gods watching over him,
you can bet on that. This family hasn't fought its last
fight, not by a long measure. Come, my lady.

OLYMPUS

Athena is looking down towards earth.

ZEUS

Athena, what are you gazing at now, or need I ask?

ATHENA

Look, father. Our messenger did his work.
Calypso releases Odysseus from her keep.

ZEUS

I find it doesn't do to look down too much like that.
Gives one a bad neck.

ATHENA

Zeus prefers to turn a blind eye. Is that it?

ZEUS

Zeus prefers a quiet life.

ATHENA

See how she dresses him in scented clothes for the trip.

ZEUS

I waste my breath.

ATHENA

And stows drink on his raft in animal skins.
One of pure water straight from the mountain spring.
One of heavy wine so he might sleep and dream.

ZEUS

If he sleeps he should tie himself to the mast.
There's trouble brewing.

ATHENA

And gives him a sack full of food. And kisses him.

ZEUS

It's of no interest to me.

ATHENA

And he kisses her back.

ZEUS

Really? So he does.

ATHENA

Then she lets him go. Lets go of his arms, his fingers, his
fingertips . . .

ZEUS

Watches him out of sight. Will he turn and wave?

ATHENA

It seems not.

ZEUS

No, the sail stiffens into shape.
He digs at the water with his oar,
and keeps the rudder tight.

Past the headland
and the jagged rocks to the west, and over the reef.

An open sea. And an open sky for the minute.
He'll be clocking the stars tonight, charting the earth by
the heavens,
watching the moon's curve.
Heading for home.

ATHENA

Except, being mighty Zeus,
it wouldn't do to watch. Right?

ZEUS

Exactly so. Or at least
we should save our viewing for when the action really
    starts.

ATHENA

What do you mean by that?

ZEUS

There's a rough ride ahead.

ATHENA

A killer whale?

ZEUS

Poseidon.

ATHENA

That's who I meant.

ZEUS

Poseidon indeed.
Look at the twitching surface of the sea.
My brother stirs in the deep.
Brooding. Biding his time.

All the signs are there.

ODYSSEUS ON HIS RAFT

ODYSSEUS
Seventeen days is it now?
Or eighteen. I lose count.
I should have notched the mast
every time it fell dark
or at every dawn.
But I've no knife or blade.
Only these fingernails,
broken and black.
Still, I'll cling to these timbers.

Holding this crude rudder tight
and using heaven's glittering chart
I've sailed in a straight line.
I'm weary, and my mind drifts,
but one thought – the thought of
home – keeps my hopes high.
Keeps me afloat. Landfall. Penelope.

Although, off to the west, the waves
seem to gallop and buck.
Don't say they're stampeding this way.
I'll hunker down, pray that they pass.

*

An hour later. The storm rages.

ODYSSEUS (*defiant, shouting to heaven*)
Is this death, then? Is it? IS THIS DEATH?
What a dirty trick. What a pitiful, pathetic,

miserable, side-winding death this is for me,
Odysseus, the unkillable genius hero of Troy,
with a hundred spears aimed at his chest
and a thousand arrows bouncing off his helmet and
    breast.
Now THAT WOULD HAVE BEEN GLORIOUS
    DEATH.
But no, it follows him over the waves, waits
till he's half-alive without armour or weapons
and crashes the whole sea onto his head.
Well, bring on the murderer. Bring on death.
Here I am. Here's a feather for your cap.
Shall I wave my arms about? Do you see me?
Let it be no secret, how miserable death
needed the force of Poseidon to kill one man.
Come ON. GIVE ME EVERYTHING YOU'VE GOT.

*A huge wave breaks over the raft. The mast splits. Odysseus
is thrown screaming into the ocean.*

OLYMPUS

Zeus and Athena follow Odysseus' progress.

ZEUS

He's a feisty one.

ATHENA

That's enough now. Call Poseidon off. Do SOMETHING.

ZEUS

No need. Look, the old sea-stirrer has turned tail.
He's had his say, made his feelings known.

ATHENA

And left Odysseus for dead.

ZEUS

No, not dead. Well, not yet, anyway.
Look, he clings to a plank of wood.

ATHENA

And what chance has he, cast adrift like that?

ZEUS

Slim. I wouldn't trade places with him, that's for sure.

But now that man and God have locked horns
and gone their separate ways,
maybe it wouldn't do any harm to er . . . how shall we
    say . . .
soothe the winds, usher them back to their quarters.

Or tug at Odysseus with a gentle hand,
steer him towards land for two or three days,
keep the sharks busy with some other scent.

[58]

The island of the Phaeacians lies ahead.
The rocks there are barbarous. Like metal teeth,
not just above the waves but underneath,
so a little swell of the sea wouldn't go amiss,
some little upsurge at the right moment in time
to land him safe on dry land. He'll be cold,
of course, and soaked to the bone, and dazed.
He'll need a path to open up through the woods,
and a place to bed down, between two olive trees
grown from the same root, for instance,
and a hugging of dry, dead leaves for a blanket.
He might sleep then, like a grain of fire
buried underground, where it can glow,
a secret spark, unnoticed, but ready to flare up.
Something of that sort wouldn't be out of turn,
if you were minded that way. Athena? Athena?

But Athena has already left.

She never did need telling twice, that one.
(*musing to himself*)
Excellent bedding, dead leaves. Dry for one thing.
Soft. Warm. Not too heavy. Make a good nest.
That's how I'd choose to hole up if it were me.

PHAEACIA

The rustle of dead leaves. Odysseus emerges from his nest.

ODYSSEUS (*jumping from his sleep, then muttering*)
What? Where have I crash-landed now?
What nowhere is this? What empty land
am I dumped on this time, like the sea's litter?

You Gods, did you give me a heart like a lemon,
the rind too thick to take on water,
bobbing endlessly from island to island?

What am I in your eyes – just sea-junk,
slewing from shore to shore with flotsam and driftwood?

(*He hears a noise.*)
What people live here? Savages. Cannibals.
Or not people at all but wild monsters.
A land of claws and fangs.
No doubt I'm already the scent of food
in the nostrils of some beast of hell,
already a taste on some rough animal's tongue.

(*He hears Nausicaa singing as she washes her clothes in
the stream.*)
Or by some miracle of fortune
an altogether gentler creature.

(*He approaches her, clearing his throat.*)
Don't jump or run away, lady.
Don't be appalled by me.

NAUSICAA (*shocked, but standing her ground*)
A thing-person, made of mud and sticks. And it speaks.

ODYSSEUS
The storm made smithereens of my raft
and the current dragged me here.
I slept in a compost of insects and leaves.
I must look like living filth in your eyes.

NAUSICAA
Like someone who crawled from a grave.

ODYSSEUS
My own, if Poseidon had his way.

NAUSICAA
You have worms in your hair.

ODYSSEUS
The sea rolled me in its jaws for twenty days . . .

NAUSICAA
You have beetles between your toes.

ODYSSEUS
. . . then spat me out. Here's where I crawled.

NAUSICAA
Naked, except for soil, although as luck would have it
you wear a sprig of leaves where men must wear clothes.

ODYSSEUS
I . . . apologize.
Especially to her whose arms
spill like milk from her shoulders.
Is it a goddess or woman I beg kindness from?

NAUSICAA
I'm Nausicaa, daughter of Alcinous and Arete,
King and Queen of the Phaeacians.

ODYSSEUS
I throw myself on your mercy.

NAUSICAA
Most visitors to our island come laden with gifts.

ODYSSEUS
I own nothing except the tongue in my head.

NAUSICAA
Most choose to approach via the harbour.

ODYSSEUS
The four winds plotted my course. I had nothing
but two arms for oars and two feet for a rudder.
(*laying on the charm*)
Would any visitor dare come with such a reckless story
and wild manner, unless his circumstances were true?
Have me arrested and thrown in chains if you wish,
but . . . if there's some glimmer of light,
if you can see the man under this muddy suit . . .

I could follow you to the palace, but lag behind,
put some time and distance between your graceful
    footsteps
and my own. It wouldn't be right for a princess
to have her brightness diminished by such a dark sight.

NAUSICAA
Very well.
But first bathe in the water, and rub yourself in oil.
And here, wear this garment I brought to wash in the
    stream.

I'll . . . look away while you dress. Then I'll walk
with damp footsteps towards home,
and you'll follow before they fade in the heat.

She giggles and leaves.

ODYSSEUS (*whispering to himself*)
Oh Athena, Goddess obscured by the sky,
if you were deaf to me while the ocean
pulverized my bones, now hear my prayer.
Let me find some courtesy among these folk,
let them show compassion to this lost soul,
let them show mercy, even love.

Let them build me a boat.

AT THE PALACE OF THE PHAEACIANS

A supper is taking place.

ALCINOUS

And you found him hiding in a pit, is that right?

NAUSICAA

In a nest of leaves where he'd curled up for the night.

ARETE

Was he fashionably dressed? Was he suitably attired?

NAUSICAA

No, mother, he was nude.

ARETE

He was what?

NAUSICAA

Stark naked, except for leaves that had stuck with sweat,
and insects and bugs that crawled in his tangled hair,
and berries that had burst their redness against his
    skin . . .

ALCINOUS

We see the image clearly, thank you, daughter.

ARETE

A bog man wearing nothing but weeds.
And you invited him here?

NAUSICAA

I took pity. I gave him a cloak.

ARETE

He's come to murder us in our beds.

NAUSICAA

And oil to soothe his tired and aching limbs.

ARETE

Tell her, Alcinous. Tell your daughter
he means to put a knife in our ribs.
A stranger, come to trick his way into our house,
and she gives him the key.

ALCINOUS

Sounds like you acted in haste, Nausicaa.

NAUSICAA

I followed my instincts, just as I was taught.

ALCINOUS

Your instincts? Are you sure it wasn't your heart?

NAUSICAA

There's something about this man, father,
something more than meets the eye,
something elemental, naked, raw . . .

ARETE

I think we've already established that.

NAUSICAA

Well, see for yourself.

*A whispering silence descends as Odysseus enters the hall
and approaches the top table.*

ODYSSEUS

Your royal highnesses. Merciful princess.

ALCINOUS (*clearing his throat*)
We ... er ...
We expected some kind of walking, talking shrub.
A raspberry patch with arms and legs.
But from our first report you've undergone a change.
Speak up, stranger.

ODYSSEUS
Your daughter found me in a filthy, rotten heap
but gave me these robes, and oil for my wounds,
and more oils to bring the shine back to my skin.
The lamp of charity burns brightly in her heart.

ARETE
We won't be hoodwinked by flattery.

NAUSICA
Mother, give him a chance.

ODYSSEUS
No, your mother is right.
Even in these borrowed clothes I do no justice to this
   noble house.

So I'll be as blunt as I dare.
I'll be as crude as I am bare
under this ill-fitting gown.
I'll be as truthful as flesh and bone,
which is all that I am now
and which is all that I own.

I am ...
(*with great boldness and courage*)
I am Odysseus. I AM ODYSSEUS,
son of Laertes, known the world over
for cunning and guile and strength of mind.

Odysseus – a hero of Troy.
My fame is written in the heavens,
and my fate too,
and my wife is Penelope,
and my son is Telemachus,
and my home is Ithaca,
but somewhere in the clockwork of islands and time and
    Gods, I'm lost.

Nymphs have held me back.
Armies have held me back.
Witches have held me back.
Sea monsters have held me back.
The one-eyed mumbling Cyclops,
the mind-melting songs of the sirens,
the deep narcotic of the lotus flower,
the prophecies of the dead,
whirlpools, clashing rocks . . .

No man loves his country or his family
more than me – the heart is a magnet,
it spins, and finds its true north, and pulls.
It tugs. Even while I sleep it tugs and tugs,
so homesickness is a permanent hurt,
a soreness, a physical tenderness – a bruise.

But the heart isn't a boat.
This heart alone won't sail me home,
and somewhere in this mad, wild, hurling clockwork
of islands and time and Gods, I'm lost.

NAUSICAA
My feelings were right. This man is set apart.
Bring him a seat.
Sit him close to the hearth and the warmth.

[67]

ARETE

    I advise caution. This is all moving very fast.

ALCINOUS

    We don't welcome strangers into our midst casually,
    Odysseus, but your speech persuades me . . .

ARETE

    He should be telling all this to the magistrate.

ALCINOUS

    Finish your story.
    If it rings true we'll carry you home to your journey's end.

ODYSSEUS

    It would take an age to tell.

ALCINOUS

    Take all the time you need. We'll listen and wait.

    Put a drink in his hand. SILENCE IN THE ROOM.
    Let nobody break the long, winding thread of his
       thoughts.
    Now, cast backwards, Odysseus, to where that strand
       begins.

ODYSSEUS (*composing himself*)

    It begins in glory, then tells of all the pain
    and misery the Gods have dreamed up for me since.

    We sailed from Troy, victorious.
    Achaeans with no thoughts other than home:
    Ithaca – the outstretched arms
    of its bay – our families – their love.
    The wind pushed us to Ismarus,
    land of the Cicones.
    We plundered the city, took meat

and wine and women and grain
to be shared equally among the men.
Then I ordered the retreat:
'Leave the rest. Back to the boats, everyone. Back to the
    coast.'

But my army was boggle-eyed
with treats, went on slaughtering
the plentiful flocks and herds,
and while they butchered and ate
and slept, the enemy grew,
drew strength from further afield,
gathered all night in the dark
then attacked out of the dawn mist,
cut us down like stalks,
flattened us into the battlefields.
Six men from every crew were lost,
the rest of us skedaddled in the boats.
Sick with grief, we saluted our dead,
then swung our oars into the water
and rowed and rowed and rowed . . .

II

ODYSSEUS AND HIS ARMY AT SEA

EURYLOCHUS
You sent for me.

ODYSSEUS
Any signs of landfall? Any omens?

EURYLOCHUS
No nesting birds to speak of,
but plenty of leaves in the sea, and a morning haze,
and two river-dolphins yesterday. We must be close.

ODYSSEUS
Nine days now.

EURYLOCHUS
Nine not counting today.

ODYSSEUS
How are the supplies?

EURYLOCHUS
Some boats low on water on account of what was spilt
when we pushed off in all that mayhem.
Some boats low on food.

ODYSSEUS
And the men?

EURYLOCHUS
Grumbling like dogs. Nothing new in that.
Want to find land soon so they can light a fire – cook up a
    hot meal.
They say they're sick of pecking at raw flesh.
They say they're not crows.

ODYSSEUS
No more dead?

EURYLOCHUS
No more. The Cicones weren't aiming to wound. They
knew how to kill.

ODYSSEUS
We brought it on ourselves, Eurylochus.
We should have taken what we needed and no more.
Instead of gorging on mutton and beef.
We got what we deserved. We were animals.

EURYLOCHUS
When you've been away from home so long,
when you've prowled from one skirmish to the next,
when you stink of the world – that's how it feels.
These men need to get home. They're turning wild.

SAILOR (off)
LAND.

ODYSSEUS
Who calls out?

EURYLOCHUS
The front boat, away in the mist.
(to the front boat)
Shout again.

SAILOR (off)
Land ahead, and a harbour, and sand to beach in.

ODYSSEUS (shouting to the other boats)
Follow their wake. Follow their wake.
(to Eurylochus)
We'll take on water,

make a fire for the night, give sacrifice and prayer,
roast the best of the meat.
And send a party of three men inland –
see what people live there – people like us, perhaps –
and if there are breads or crops to be had.
Then we'll sail first thing next day.

EURYLOCHUS (*repeating the order*)
Follow their wake.

THE LOTUS EATERS

*Next morning, on the coast of a tropical paradise, with
exotic birds calling from the interior and waves washing
gently against the shore.*

ODYSSEUS

A bright morning, a waiting sea and a friendly wind. All
prepared?

EURYLOCHUS

All the pots and bags filled and all stowed.

ODYSSEUS

And all the men counted and numbered?

EURYLOCHUS

Except for the three you sent inland.

ODYSSEUS

What time did they set out?

EURYLOCHUS

Just before dusk last night.

ODYSSEUS

And no sign of them since?

EURYLOCHUS

Not a sniff.

ODYSSEUS

Which way did they go?

EURYLOCHUS

That steep path by the cliff. See, where those flowers
bloom.

ODYSSEUS

You mean the . . . which flowers? Not those?

EURYLOCHUS

Beautiful, aren't they? And the smell.
I'd swear the scent of them was making me quite light-
    headed last night.
I dreamed of when I was a boy, in my father's garden . . .

ELPENOS (*calls out*)

My beautiful leader. My beautiful friends.

EURYLOCHUS

Here they are. Call off the search party.

ODYSSEUS

Bring me a rope from the ship.

EURYLOCHUS

I thought you wanted to sail. Now you want to hunt?

EURYBATES

Come here by the flowers. Come and feast with us.

ANTIPHUS

Odysseus, bliss to you, my king, bliss, my friend.

EURYLOCHUS

Are they drunk? Have they found wine?

ODYSSEUS

Not wine, something far more potent.
Those are lotus flowers. The fruit and the seed
when taken on the tongue . . . they say
the gates of perception are flung wide and the spirit soars.
But when the feeling dies, the soul enters a chasm.

Worse than that – if the lotus gets into our blood
we'll lose all judgement and sense;

we need minds quicker than knives and sharper than
     swords
or we'll never reach home. Fetch the rope.

The three scouts approach Odysseus.

ELPENOS
     Odysseus, come taste what we've found.
     Honey of all honey. Sugar of all sweetness.

ANTIPHUS
     My king, you have landed us in paradise.

EURYBATES
     Such smoothness enters the mind.
     Colours are endless and limitless.

ANTIPHUS
     Ask me what I feel, my beautiful comrade.
     I feel a vast, velvet pleasantness.

EURYBATES
     I feel purple ecstasy.

ANTIPHUS
     I feel harmony. The golden harmony.

ODYSSEUS
     Take nothing from them. Don't even smell their breath.

ELPENOS
     The rapture of all mankind uncurls in me.
     The Gods are in my bloodstream.
     All the joy of existence, the rush of life . . .

EURYBATES
     And the wonder, the wonder, the wonder . . .
     Every nerve in my body vibrates in orgasm . . .

ODYSSEUS

Rope these three and haul them back to the ship.

ELPENOS

Ropes. Not ropes. Why ropes, Odysseus?

ODYSSEUS

And search their pockets for those fatal plants.

ANTIPHUS (*beginning to panic*)

Odysseus, comrade, beautiful friend, don't pain me.
It's all here and it's all free.

ODYSSEUS

Be quiet. Pull yourself together.

ANTIPHUS

Taste it for yourself – the essence of it.
Don't pain me, Odysseus? Odysseus?
Give me my flower.
GIVE ME MY FLOWER.

ELPENOS (*weeping like a child*)

It isn't yours to take away.
You've got your own Gods, why can't we worship the
    flower,
float in the fever of its pollen for ever?

ODYSSEUS

Give me that stuff. Throw it on the floor. All of it.

ANTIPHUS (*sobbing*)

You destroyers, you killjoys, you assassins, you
    executioners . . .
This is rape. This is THE MURDER OF LOVE.
This isn't FAIR.

EURYBATES
  Get these ropes off. NOW.
  YOU BASTARDS.

ODYSSEUS
  Turn out his pockets.

EURYBATES
  Leave my pockets alone.
  Those flowers are mine, mine,
  mine, mine, mine, mine, mine (*dissolves in tears*)

*The three men are hauled back to the ship protesting and
weeping pathetically.*

ODYSSEUS (*shouting after them*)
  Tie them on deck until they stop jabbering.
  And wash your hands in the sea. I want no pollen
  of that crazy species dusting the air
  or spiking the wine or seasoning the food,
  or taking root under someone's boot.
  I won't carry it home.

  Scrub them of every spore.

IN THE PALACE OF THE PHAEACIANS

ODYSSEUS

The wind rose, hauling us forward.
The drugged men wailed,
shivered until their bones rattled.
They puked and went pale. Then sat and stared,
their eyes sinking into their heads
like jewels thrown overboard.
Landfall came quickly. Before we knew it
the boats had run aground on a shelf,
whispered to a halt in soft sand. Land,
but not home. We'd heard the folklore
of that place, rumours of a one-eyed freak
roaming the cliffs. Cyclops – Poseidon's weird son.
We should have steered clear, but the thought of food
and fresh milk took us straight to his cave.

CYCLOPS

ODYSSEUS

This way, but no sudden noises.

You, man, go through those rocks and peer in.

ELPENOS

Has he really only one eye?

EURYBATES

That's what they say. So why should we fear – he's already
half blind.

What do you say, Polites?

POLITES

One eye only, but it's as wide and as deep and as clear
as a barrel of rain. So he'll see us all right, if he's in range.

ELPENOS

If his eye's so big there can't be much room for his ears.

EURYBATES

So we can sneak up on him while he looks the other way,
and he won't hear a thing!

POLITES

There's room all right, because his head is as big as a
boulder.

Now pipe down, before we find out.

SHIPMATE (*from the mouth of the cave*)

It's all clear. Nobody home.

POLITES

Are you sure?

SHIPMATE

Cave's empty – apart from the smell.

But these buckets aren't, and neither are these stalls.

Come and feast your eyes on this lot.

They run over to the mouth of the cave. The bleating of lambs and kids can be heard.

EURYBATES

Cornucopia. There must be five dozen heads here.

ELPENOS

Lamb *and* goat. We'll stuff our faces tonight.

ANTIPHUS

And snouters. I can hear them hissing and spitting on the fire already.

EURYBATES

What's in the buckets?

ELPENOS

Milk, is it?

EURYBATES

More like cheese, or whey.

ELPENOS

Well, whey – hey! It's like he knew we were coming and laid on a feast.

Let's get everything back to the boats.

ODYSSEUS

No, we should wait.

ELPENOS

Wait for what, Odysseus? Sir?

ODYSSEUS

He might make us welcome here. Give us this food as
    a gift.

EURYBATES

He's a one-eyed monster who eats people alive.
I'm not hanging around to sample his hospitality.

ANTIPHUS

Me neither. Here, help me herd these sheep.

ODYSSEUS

I SAID WE WILL WAIT.
We're not savages. We're Achaeans of Ithaca.
Men of our word.
We're not rampaging from shore to shore
without cause,
we're making the long journey home
after a just war.
Get your minds above your bellies for a minute.
Greed and gluttony
lost us half our men against the Cicones.
You, make a fire.
You, take modest portions of cheese and milk
into the cave.
We'll wait for our host. Today we'll be civilized.

The men grumble but follow his instructions.

Everyone into the cave.

*

*Later. Around a crackling fire, the men sit chatting in the
echoing cave, waiting the return of Cyclops.*

ELPENOS

What about you?

EURYBATES

What about me?

ELPENOS

What's the first thing you'll do when you get home?

EURYBATES

Obvious, isn't it?

The rest of the men laugh and whistle.

ELPENOS

All right, what's the second thing?

EURYBATES

I'll probably do it again.

More laughter and whistling.

ANTIPHUS

Tell you what I'll do. I've got a little plot of land above
the cliff. It's not much but it feeds me and the family.
It's probably gone to seed by now. Well, first I'll build
the walls back up, make it all trim and tidy. Then I'll
put a crop in the soil . . . barley or wheat. Then at dusk,
I'll say a prayer to Zeus, and throw a stone in the sea,
and swear on that stone never, ever, ever to set foot on
a boat again. I'm going to plant myself in that field, and
I'm going to take root.

ELPENOS

I'll drink to that.

EURYBATES (*proposing a toast*)

To Ithaca!

ALL

To Ithaca!

ANTIPHUS

Then I'll get off home to the wife for a bit of what you
were talking about.

They all roar with laughter.

SHIPMATE

Something approaches.

ODYSSEUS

Is it him?

SHIPMATE

He's . . . he's enormous.

ODYSSEUS

Everyone right to the back of the cave,
and total silence.

SHIPMATE

He's enormous. Enormous!

ODYSSEUS

Hold on to your thoughts, watchman,
or I'll put my fist through your skull and hold them for
you.
Now quiet everyone.

*The Cyclops arrives at the mouth of the cave, grunting and
snuffling. He babbles and mutters to himself, then snooks,
clears his throat and spits out a ball of snot.*

ANTIPHUS (*whispering*)

In heaven's name – he's inhuman.

EURYBATES

Look at those hands. He'll mangle us.

ELPENOS

We're done for, we're pulp.

SHIPMATE

I told you. He's enormous.

ODYSSEUS

Shut it. All of you, before he hears us.

CYCLOPS

Yahn,

Tayhn,

Tether,

Mether,

Mimph,

Hither,

Lither,

Danver,

Dic . . .

EURYBATES

What's he doing? What's he saying?

ODYSSEUS

He's counting his flock into the pen.

EURYBATES

What language is he speaking?

CYCLOPS

Yahndic,

Tayhndic,

Tetherdic,

Metherdic,

Mimphit,
Yahn-a-mimphit,
Tayhn-a-mimphit,
Tether-a-mimphit,
Mether-a-mimphit . . .

ANTIPHUS
It's baby-talk if you ask me. Gobbledygook language.

CYCLOPS (*hearing them*)
WHAT? Grokells! Infesters!
Who squatting in Cyclops' cave?
Who dodging and skulking in shadows in Cyclops' cave?

ODYSSEUS (*speaking up from the back*)
Pardon us.
We're men of Ithaca, blown off course
by cruel winds, at the mercy of the sea.
We fetched up here by chance. We mean
no harm and hope you might welcome us
as strangers in a strange land. We offer
the hand of friendship and our word.
We are true men, respecters of the Gods.

CYCLOPS
Gods!
(*He bellows with laughter.*)
Cyclops farts in Gods' faces. Cyclops pisses on Gods' feet.
Cyclops does whatever Cyclops please.
(*in a clumsy attempt at cunning*)
So, er, where did Ithaca men land them ship?

POLITES (*whispering*)
Don't tell him. He'll find it and crush it.

EURYLOCHUS

Odysseus, throw him off the scent.

ODYSSEUS

Our ship was wrecked.
We entered the bay.
We swam for our lives.
Myself and the men that you see
are all that's left.

*Cyclops mumbles and muses to himself, then giggles, then
mumbles and giggles some more.*

CYCLOPS

Cyclops lonely. Cyclops on his own.

ELPENOS

Aw, look at him, he's just a big kid.

EURYBATES

He's grinning. You're right. He's a big soft lump really.

Cyclops giggles and laughs. The men begin to laugh.

ANTIPHUS

He likes us. He thinks we're his friends – big dumb
animal. Come on, let's help ourselves to this fodder.

ODYSSEUS

Wait a second, let me talk to him some more.

ANTIPHUS

It's fine. Hey, one-eye, how about me and you get our
teeth stuck into that slab of cheese over there? I'll have
the first bite . . .

Cyclops grabs the man and devours him. The other men scream and shout as Antiphus is crushed and eaten. Cyclops slabbers and drools and burps as he gobbles his victim, crunching his bones between his teeth.

ODYSSEUS
Everyone, get right back into the crag where he can't reach us.

POLITES
He's closing the door – we're trapped.

ELPENOS
We should have cut and run while we had the chance.
Now he's going to eat us alive one by one.

ODYSSEUS
Get right into the crack there.
Pack down, make room for everyone.

ELPENOS
He'll pluck us out with those long, gangling arms.
Where is he now?

POLITES
Pacing around the cave, looking this way.

CYCLOPS
GRRRRRNNNNNNNNAAAWWWWWW.

ELPENOS
He's got us right where he wants us.
We're dead meat. He'll just reach in and grab us.

ODYSSEUS
This fissure's too narrow for him
and we'll guard the entrance with spears.
We'll wait in this bolt-hole until morning.

ELPENOS

Why, so he can eat us for breakfast?

ODYSSEUS

Settle down and rest. We're safe here.
Be quiet and let me think.

CYCLOPS

GGGRRRRNNNNAAAWWWWWWW.

Out of breath, the men cower at the back of the cave.

EURYBATES

Poor old Antiphus.
I don't suppose he'll be needing that field of his any more.

*

Morning in the cave. Cyclops is snoring. Sheep are bleating.

EURYBATES

My arm's gone to sleep.

ELPENOS

Move your leg. Your foot's right in my face.

ODYSSEUS

Watchman, can you see anything?

SHIPMATE

He's still asleep. He's got blood on his chin and bones
stuck in his teeth.

EURYLOCHUS

A hundred of us couldn't move that boulder from the
entrance.
He's bunged the hole. We're trapped like flies in a bottle.

ODYSSEUS

All right, listen to me.
Who has wine left in their sacks?
Pour it all into this one bag.
Let's see if Cyclops here can handle his drink.

ELPENOS

He's already scoffed poor Antiphus. Now you're giving
him wine to whet his appetite for the rest of us.

EURYBATES

We should drink it ourselves – at least we'd die happy.

ODYSSEUS

Hand it to Polites and Eurylochus.
Trust me, this is our only means of escape.

Odysseus emerges from the back of the cave and approaches the stirring Cyclops.

ODYSSEUS

Wake up. Here's a peace offering from the men of Ithaca.

Cyclops grumbles.

ODYSSEUS

Good wine, strong wine.
It tastes better than men's blood.
Drink this instead, and let us go. Here, catch.

He throws Cyclops the wine sack.

CYCLOPS

What Ithaca man name?

ODYSSEUS

My name? You want my name?
Nobody, that's what they call me.

Nobody's my name.

CYCLOPS

Nobody? Huh, Nobody. Cyclops drink wine. Cyclops eat
Nobody last. Cyclops save Nobody for pudding. Ha!

*He laughs and begins guzzling the wine. Odysseus returns to
his men.*

ELPENOS

Well, that was a fat lot of good. Now he's got the wine
and us. If Odysseus ever goes into the bartering
business he'll be bankrupt in a week.

Cyclops starts gurgling and singing to himself.

ODYSSEUS

Listen to him – he's a stranger to wine.
He doesn't know the boozy fumes of the grape.
Wait till it floods through his veins,
wait till it loosens the knot of his brain.

Cyclops burps and laughs and glugs more of the wine.

Eurylochus, Polites.
And you, man, and you, and you.
See that log in the ogre's fire – the longer one?
See its pointed end – it glows red with heat.
Come with me when I give the word, hoist it
onto my shoulder, then push from behind.
I'll aim it into the soul of that creature's life.

POLITES

Into his heart to kill him?

ODYSSEUS

No, comrades, into his eye.

We'll blind him, but we need him alive.

Cyclops is humming to himself and laughing.

Follow me.
Hush now. More stealth.
Softly – here by the fire.
That's the one.
See the tip – like a branding iron.
Lift it after three.
One . . . two . . . three.
(*straining under the weight*) Ngg . . .
Forward.
Steady it.
Hold it there.

Hey, Cyclops, over here. Are you awake? Are you open
eyed?

CYCLOPS

Who shout Cyclops?
Nobody man. Cyclops hungry now for Nobody.

ODYSSEUS

Here I am, in the shadow.
(*to his men*)
Look how his pupil dilates. Wait till it stretches wide.
(*to Cyclops*)
See me now? Here by the rock. Here's Nobody for you.

CYCLOPS

GGGGGGGRRRRRRRNNNAAWWWWWWWW.

ODYSSEUS

Do you see me? Do you see Nobody?

ELPENOS

He'll smash us to pieces.

EURYBATES

The Gods have deserted us. He's got the jaw of a lion.

ELPENOS

And the teeth of a shark.

POLITES

This is doomed, Odysseus.

ODYSSEUS

Hold your position. Here he comes.

CYCLOPS

Cyclops eat now,
chew Nobody's flesh.
bite out Nobody's heart,
tear off Nobody's head. . . . GGNNNAWWWW.

ODYSSEUS

NOW!

The men run forward and drive the burning stake into Cyclops' eye. He lets out an ear-splitting scream. The stake fizzes as his eye burns and boils.

Drive. Drive. Drive.
Ram it all the way home . . .

CYCLOPS

NNNNNAAAAARRGGHHHHHHHH . . .

ODYSSEUS

Now twist and gouge,
now heave, heave, heave, heave . . .

IN THE PALACE OF THE PHAEACIANS

ODYSSEUS
    . . . heave, heave.
    Then all the men came and added their weight,
    hammered that burning stake into his head,
    and when the eyeball burst we were soaked in ink,
    and the lens crunched and cracked like splintering ice,
    and the lashes and eyebrows flared like burning grass,
    and we leaned, and heaved, and forced it further in
    until the retina sheared, and the optic nerve
    spat and seared and spasmed and fused in the heat.
    All the while he screamed into the cave,
    roared his pain into the booming, echoing rock,
    so loud that other one-eyed monsters on the island
    came to listen. They gathered outside, more curious
    than concerned, and called, 'Hey, you in there,
    what's all the fuss and palaver? Who's giving you grief?'
    And Cyclops, writhing in pain, his head in flames,
    shouted, 'Nobody. Nobody hurts Cyclops. Nobody.'

    So they shrugged their shoulders and padded off home.
    A master-stroke on my part, and it worked.
    When we drew out the stake it was like a bung,
    like a cork, like a plug – blood spurted and plumed,
    but I didn't finish him off, the thick-headed brute. Why?
    He'd rolled a stone across the cave's mouth, blocking the
        gap,
    a stone so vast that he alone could shift it from the hole.
    And this was the whole point of my ingenious plan.
    The flock were cowering away from the noise and flames.
    Twines and twisted willow-strands littered the floor.

Each man lashed himself tight under a fat ram,
and two other rams were tethered alongside
to shield him at the flanks as he dangled and clung on.
Then they ambled forward, tottered over the stone floor,
bleated to be let out of the cave for water and pasture,
and Cyclops, even with a smoking hole instead of an eye,
was still a shepherd at heart, so he rolled away the rock,
opened the mouth of the cave and counted them out,
stroking their backs as they wandered into the light:
'Mether, Tether, Mimph, Hither, Lither, Anver, Danver . . .'
The ignorant swine, he released them one at a time,
each big ram with one of my men slung under its gut.
And I was the last man to escape, suspended beneath
the cockiest ram of the lot, my fingers twisted
into the deep shag of his coat, my feet stirruped
in the swags of elastic skin to the inside of his leg.

Once on the boats with the men and the flock
and the buckets of cheeses and barrels of milk,
I goaded the Cyclops with taunts, and he hurled rocks
from the cliff but they only caused ripples
that pushed us further to sea. The wide open sea.

And the men cheered and laughed until light . . .
when it dawned on us that nothing had changed.

Still lost, still famished-hearted, still years from home,
but now with Poseidon fuming and writhing below us,
plotting revenge for blinding his one-eyed son.

That act was to haunt us. From then on
we were marked men, locked on a collision course
with the God of the Sea. He lurked in the depths,
a constant presence. We sensed him under the waves.
The boat shivered when he stirred. And if we'd have known

the chain of events we'd set in place, the cruelty
and agony that stretched ahead, year after year,
the horror and terror and sadness and loss still to come –
   who knows,
perhaps we'd have chosen to die right there, in the black
   cave,
out of sight of heaven and without sound.

With our fate now in the hands of the Gods
we drifted on wind and current, hoping again,
hoping against hope, praying, looking for land.

IN THE PALACE OF THE PHAEACIANS

Stunned silence follows Odysseus' story.

ALCINOUS

Odysseus, yours is a fantastical tale . . .

NAUSICAA

Such adventure and excitement, and such bravery.
Hearing it causes a drum-roll in my heart.

ARETE

Breathtaking all right. Flabbergasting in fact.
Blinding the Cyclops with a burning branch,
then escaping tied to a ram – do we believe this man?

ODYSSEUS

Courteous King Alcinous, graceful Queen Arete,
Princess Nausicaa, who salvaged me in the woods,
and you Phaeacians, who tolerate my company,

what I've told you so far is only the start, fabulous
as it might seem. The mind-altering lotus plant,
the puddle-eyed Cyclops with his taste for flesh –
there's enough weirdness and terror right there
to fill a man's days, you might think, and you'd be right.
But they're nothing compared to what lay ahead.

Let me explain how outrageous twists of fortune and fate
led me to your island in this ruined state.

ALCINOUS

You have our permission and our attention.

NAUSICAA

We're entranced, enraptured, aren't we, father?
So, you blinded the Cyclops with a red-hot pile-driver,
left him shaking his fist at the top of the cliff . . .

ODYSSEUS

Seething, cursing, tearing up rocks and lumps of earth
to hurl at the ship, calling his father, Poseidon, to rise
from the deep and clatter us, feed us to the fish.

But we rode out the storm, and landed by chance
on the Island of Aeolia, home of good Aeolus,
whose palace shines like a mirage above the sea,
whose halls and rooms are thick – night and day –
with the smell of freshly roasted beasts and fish and game.

He hosted us royally. Not one of our needs went
    unattended,
and before we sailed he gave me a cloth bag, tightly
    strung,
with the south wind, the north, and the wind from the
    east
bundled inside, so not one breath could blow us off
    course,
but the west wind he kept free to puff us gently along.

Yet his kindly thoughts were wasted on us.
Nine days on, we gave in to our weaknesses and faults.

THE BAG OF WIND

SHIPMATE

Land. I see land.

ELPENOS

I see it too.

EURYBATES

Where?

ELPENOS

To the left. Look, can't you see the trees?

EURYBATES

No. Where? Yes, now I see it, through the mist.

ELPENOS

And fires. Men setting fires at dusk.

Wait a second, look at that promontory. Look, look.

EURYBATES

He's right – see the shape of the bay and the bluff. It can't
   be. It can't be.

ELPENOS

Ithaca – oh, make a sacrifice to Zeus. We'll slaughter the
   proudest animal on the island as soon as we set foot on
   solid ground. We're home. WE'RE HOME!

There is jubilation amongst the men.

EURYLOCHUS

All eyes to the port side.
Praise be to mighty Zeus who returns us home.
Odysseus? Odysseus?

ODYSSEUS (*at the other end of the boat, to himself*)
I see it, my men. I saw it an hour ago.
Wouldn't allow myself to believe it.
Willing it, trying to make it materialize.
Stared so hard and long I'm hypnotized,
dazed by it. Ithaca – I hardly dare say it
in case it breaks like a dream and disappears.

(*to the men*)
An hour or so until we put in. Make ready.
And scrub yourselves, and scour every deck.
Shout the orders across the boats. Pride, men.
We won't return like ragamuffins and louts.
Stitch every tear. Cover your wounds.
Comb the salt from your beards, and smile!
We'll come home as handsome as we left,
and with honour, and with Troy to our name.

EURYLOCHUS
Odysseus, sir. Come and drink with the crew.

ODYSSEUS
No, I won't. Suddenly I'm . . . overcome.
As if every muscle and nerve
has been stretched and strained for twenty years.
Twenty years hardly daring to sleep or even blink.
I feel . . . fantastically tired.

EURYLOCHUS
But you can relax now, we're home.

ODYSSEUS
I'll sleep for a while. Wake me as we land.

EURYLOCHUS

I will, I'll be ready with clean clothes and a meal.

*

Later, approaching the shore of Ithaca.

SHIPMATE

Is there a drink there for me?

ELPENOS

Help yourself.

SHIPMATE

I will indeed. Well, here's to home, and Odysseus.

EURYBATES

I'll drink to the first all right, but not the second.

SHIPMATE

You won't raise a toast to your captain and king,
who guided us back to our own coast,
saved us from certain death time and time again?

ELPENOS

It was luck. He's just a lucky son of a . . .

SHIPMATE

Watch your tongue or you'll be shark-meat, friend.

EURYBATES

Let him speak. Because he's right, isn't he? Look at him
now, asleep on a plump cushion, adored the world over,
worshipped like a God. And why – because fortune
smiles on him – that's all. Not like me. If I fell in a
barrel of bosoms I'd come out sucking my thumb. He's
the golden one.

SHIPMATE

He's got foresight and acumen and charisma.

ELPENOS

That isn't all he's got.

SHIPMATE

Explain yourself.

ELPENOS

Booty. Plunder. The spoils of war – that's what I'm talking about.

EURYBATES

Exactly.

ELPENOS

All the swag that he's bringing home from Troy, while us lot who stood and scrapped on the front line come home penniless and broken.

SHIPMATE

It's nothing more than he's entitled to.
It's appropriate to his position.

ELPENOS

It's greed. Self-indulgence.

EURYBATES

Look what happened only nine days ago. Aeolus gives him a bag of goodies which he squirrels away. More riches for him and two fingers to the rest of us. Well, I won't stand for it any longer.

SHIPMATE

Don't do anything rash, not now. We'll soon be in port.

ELPENOS

Aye, soon be shambling down that gangplank like
paupers, while Odysseus saunters home with a king's
ransom. Fetch that bag!

SHIPMATE

This is very irregular.

EURYBATES

No, it's equality. Fairness. Where did he hide it?

ELPENOS

In that locker. No, the bottom one. Under the shelf.

SHIPMATE

I'll have to inform him – it's my duty.

ELPENOS

Go on then, go running to him. Or why not have a little
squint in this bag? See what you're missing. See if
there's anything you fancy.

SHIPMATE

No, I . . . Well, I . . .

ELPENOS

A little look won't harm, will it?

SHIPMATE (*gulps*)

Just a peep perhaps, no crime in that. Since you're
opening it anyway.

EURYBATES

Here we go. It's a bit light. No precious stones, that's for
sure.

ELPENOS

Pass it here. Whoa! It's squirming. Must be an animal.

Some rare species bred for its perfume – worth a
fortune, I bet. Whooaaa! Keep still, you crazy ferret.
Anyone got a knife?

SHIPMATE

Let me, let me! I mean, you can borrow mine if you want.

ELPENOS

Hold it straight while I slit the drawstring.
(*struggling with it*)
What is it tied with, wire? Ah, nearly there. One last . . .
GOT IT.

*There is a huge rush of air, building up and up, as if a
hurricane has been let loose on the ship. The winds of the
south, east and north whip themselves into a frenzy.*

ODYSSEUS (*running towards them*)
NO! CLOSE THE BAG. CLOSE THE BAG.

SHIPMATE

Odysseus. Help us.

ODYSSEUS

Who opened the bag? Who freed the winds?

SHIPMATE

The men – they wanted their fair share.

ODYSSEUS (*incredulous*)
Fair share of what?

SHIPMATE

Whatever it held. They wanted some for themselves.

ODYSSEUS (*full of bitterness and fury*)
Well, now they have it. Tell them to hold on for dear life,
and tell them to weep.

SHIPMATE

Why should they cry?

ODYSSEUS

Because the winds sweep us along now,
sweep us north and south and west.
And Ithaca lies east.

SHIPMATE

But we're almost home. I saw trees, landmarks, fires
burning above the coast. It was close enough to touch.

ODYSSEUS

But you were thieves instead. Now wave goodbye.

The wind-speed increases, howling across the ship.

SHIPMATE

No. No. (*screams*) ITHACA. ITHACA . . .

ODYSSEUS (*almost to himself*)

Tell it to the stars. Save your tonsils.
Ithaca sails away. She can't hear you.

IN THE PALACE OF THE PHAEACIANS

NAUSICAA
> I can't bear it.
> To have smelt the pine cones of your own country,
> only to be yanked away. Such cruelty.

ALCINOUS
> Weren't you tempted to dive in and swim for it?

ODYSSEUS
> In that maelstrom
> I would have drowned instantly, disappeared completely.
> And I was half-tempted, for that very reason, to be shot
> of the whole thing, to shut out the torture, to end it
> there and then. After all, the Gods can't torment the
>   dead,
> can they? But instincts took over. The will to live –
> it's an impulse that can't be repressed. And I took
>   comfort
> in one thing: the winds whipped up such surf and
>   spindrift
> that Ithaca couldn't be seen. How sad would that have
>   been –
> to watch the home fires of my home town receding?
>
> No, desolated but too numb to be defeated, I clung on.
> We were blown back to where we'd begun, the Island
> of Aeolia, but this time Aeolus shunned us, turned us
>   away,
> saying, 'The Gods never want you to rest, Odysseus,
> there's a hex on your head. I shouldn't help you again,
> they might turn their anger on me. Get out of my life.'

NAUSICAA
So you sailed again? Where to next?

ODYSSEUS
To where the breeze took us – Laestrygonia.
That land of endless sun, with less than a hair's breadth
between dusk and daybreak, where night-time
is the split-second blink of heaven's eyelid.

It should have been a routine stop for supplies,
so I moored my vessel some distance off at sea.
The fleet sailed into the narrow-jawed harbour
and a search party followed a twist of smoke
to where a thick-limbed girl drew water from a well.
Follow me home, she told them. They followed.
In the halls of the Laestrygonians sat her mother,
a giant toad of a woman. She called her husband,
Antiphates, king of those people. I say people,
I mean people-eaters. He snatched one of my men,
swallowed him whole. The rest ran for the boats
but the cannibals followed, hundreds now,
stoning the boats from the headland
and hunting my men like spear-fishermen.
'Row for your lives, row for your lives,' I bellowed.
I hauled three or four floundering men aboard,
slit the mooring ropes with my sword
and my boat pulled clear. But not the others.

Not one ship made it out of that harbour.

If twelve ships sailed from Troy for Ithaca,
now we were one vessel alone, and heartbroken.

Behind us, planks, clothing and limbs
floated randomly on the crimson ocean.

We pin-balled between islands again, barely conscious.
We were lost utterly. Knew nothing. Cared even less.

But after slaughter came humiliation and ignominy:
the wind delivered us into the lap of Circe.

CIRCE

Odysseus and the last of his men on land on Aeaea. They are seated around a campfire, eating a meal on the beach.

ELPENOS

This is the sweetest food.

EURYBATES

Yes, stag. I feel big when I've eaten stag.

ELPENOS

I know what you mean – as if you've eaten its spirit as well. As if the ghost of the stag enters the blood, making you fearless and proud. Like you're the king of the woods.

EURYBATES

I just meant it's very filling, that's all.

ELPENOS

Oh, I see.

EURYBATES

I was starving. I could have eaten the antlers as well. Very rich, though.

ELPENOS

Yes.

EURYBATES

Who killed it?

ELPENOS

Odysseus. Brought it down with one throw of the spear – thwack. Splintered its backbone. I saw him dragging it

down to the beach, hauling it on a rope made from
creepers and vines.

EURYBATES
Amazing.

ELPENOS
Yes, and he gave us the pick of the meat.

EURYBATES
Really generous.

ELPENOS
I feel terrible now after that business with the bag of wind
and everything we said.

EURYBATES
Me too.

ELPENOS
Yes, really rotten. Hey, are you leaving that rib?

EURYBATES
Have it. Very filling is stag. Very rich.

ODYSSEUS
Listen to me, men. I've been up on that crag
surveying the interior, trying to make a plan.
It's mysterious here. The plateau is dense jungle,
crammed with ancient trees that interweave
and link arms. Animal noises came to me,
but no beasts I could name from their voices.
I saw birds with feathers like flames, and plants
that swallowed insects, and lizards more like dragons
with double tongues and black smoking breath.

This is a disorienting place, no question of that.

In truth, it's hard to tell east from west,
or even dawn from dusk. The sea lies to every side.
To look for sweet water, animal flesh and fruit
we have no choice – we'll have to strike inland.

The men groan and protest.

ELPENOS

Haven't we learned our lesson by now?
Isn't there something of a pattern developing here?

POLITES

Hold your tongue.

ODYSSEUS

No, Polites, if he has something on his mind let him
   speak.

ELPENOS

I'm not saying anything, all right. It's just that . . .

EURYBATES

He's saying we should just pack up and go. Every time we
   go up country we come face to face with some bunch of
   crazies trying to cut us to shreds, or some one-eyed
   retard, or some other nightmare. Why don't we finish
   our meal, get back on the boats and sail? At least on
   the water there's only the weather to bother about.
   What's a few thunderstorms compared with a
   flesh-eating ogre, or flowers dosed with brain-addling
   drugs, or blood-sucking primitives . . .?

ODYSSEUS

So it's fear, is it? Is that what roots you to the spot?

EURYBATES

Look what's happened to us! I've got every right to be

fearful. Yes, I'm afraid, and I don't mind saying so.
(*becoming tearful*) Terrified. Shit-scared, OK? Satisfied?
You're right, I should be used to it by now. My nerves
are shot. I'm finished.

ODYSSEUS

Well, even if your cowardice shames you,
some pride is salvaged by your honesty.
It's been desperate,
it's no surprise that cracks are starting to show.

But honesty doesn't change our predicament
or release us from jeopardy. It's no use blubbing.
And we can't sail without water and food,
we might as well slit our throats here on the beach.
So we soldier on. Here's my strategy:

There's no point putting the whole party at risk.
We divide into two groups, I'll lead one
and my good lord Eurylochus the other.

EURYLOCHUS

An honour, sir.

ODYSSEUS

We draw lots. One group remains here,
the other presses forward on reconnaissance.
Any dissenting voices to that plan of action?
Good. You, man, take off your helmet
and throw in these buttons – one gold,
one silver. Eurylochus, draw your lot.

*Two buttons are thrown into a bronze helmet. Eurylochus
draws out the gold one.*

EURYLOCHUS
  Gold, sir.

ODYSSEUS
  You win – that being the noblest of the metals.
  So, stand idle here by the ships, or cut a path into the
    bush
  and carve out a name for yourself? It's your choice.

EURYLOCHUS (*obliged to take on the challenge*)
  The choice is obvious.

ODYSSEUS
  Brave Eurylochus. Take two dozen men,
  and Polites, brother in arms, go with them.

POLITES
  I will. I'm ready for a change of scene.

ODYSSEUS
  Friends, death's door yawns open for us,
  but we won't enter, not for a while yet.
  These comrades of ours are our lifeline.
  Give them the best of your arrows and spears
  and press good luck into their handshakes.

  May the Gods of good fortune smile on you.
  We'll watch and listen for signs and signals.

*

*The reconnaissance party make their way through the
wooded interior of the island.*

ELPENOS
  Ouch!

EURYBATES

What?

ELPENOS

Mosquitoes.

EURYBATES

I know, they're ravenous. I've given up counting the bites.
I've got more bites than skin.

ELPENOS

They can smell the fear. It's fear that attracts them.

EURYBATES

Well, they must be having a feast day with me and I don't
mind admitting it.

EURYLOCHUS

Caution, men. Everybody keep low for a moment.

POLITES

What is it?

EURYLOCHUS

Look, in the clearing.

POLITES

A magnificent palace. Only someone of great nobility
could live there.

ELPENOS

Or great cunning.

*A beguiling song drifts through the palace door and out
towards them.*

POLITES

Listen.

[116]

EURYLOCHUS
What is it? Music?

POLITES
Singing. Hear it?

EURYLOCHUS
A woman's voice.

POLITES
Captivating. Enthralling. Enchanting.

They listen a while longer.

POLITES
We should . . . I'll take a handful of men and approach the
gate.

EURYLOCHUS
I'll stay outside – take a look around the gardens and
grounds.

POLITES
Listen to that voice – it's angelic. Inviting us in, almost.
Anyway, we can't just go on skulking in the bushes.
We might as well take the initiative.
You others, come with me, but there's a lady at home,
so mind your manners.

*They approach the door. The singing is louder and more
beautiful than ever.*

ELPENOS
I haven't heard singing like that for years.

EURYBATES
There's no more wonderful instrument than the human

voice. My wife used to sing to me while she was cutting my hair.

ELPENOS

My daughter was the singer in our house. A little song-bird, she was. She won't be little any more. She'll have flown the nest.

POLITES

All right, make yourselves presentable, men.
Keep your weapons close to hand but no sudden moves.
We don't want a bloodbath.

He bangs on the door. The singing continues inside the house. Polites knocks again. The singer reaches the end of the song and stops. Slow, measured footsteps make their way towards the door, accompanied by the swishing hem of a long dress. The door opens.

CIRCE (*seductively*)

Hello, gentlemen.

POLITES

Forgive our intrusion.

CIRCE

What's to forgive? I can sing any time,
but it's not every day a band of men call at my door.
Were you washed ashore?

POLITES

We've been blown every which way –
will you excuse our untidy appearance?

CIRCE

I see only the potential in a man, not his blurred outline.
But don't loiter in the doorway, gentlemen. Come in.

They file into the house and are shown into a dining room.

CIRCE

Does any one of you men have an appetite?

ELPENOS

What a spread. There's enough here to feed an army.

POLITES

This is . . . an unexpected surprise.

EURYBATES

Oh, brother, I think my belly's going to leap up through
my throat and lunge for it. Er, if you'll pardon my way
of speaking, ma'am.

CIRCE

Do be seated. Don't stand on ceremony.

POLITES

And just the right number of chairs. It's as if you were
expecting us.

CIRCE

Never underestimate the foresight of the hostess.

EURYBATES

No, don't do that, Polites. And don't look a gift-horse in
the mouth either.

ELPENOS

There's wine by the gallon. And food I've never seen the
likes of. Dishes I don't even recognize.

CIRCE

You look like men of the world.
You don't look like men who'd turn down a meal
just because it was foreign or unfamiliar.

ELPENOS
Too right we wouldn't.

EURYBATES (*tucking in*)
So you keep a bit of a farm, do you? I noticed the stalls in
the walled garden.

CIRCE
I have livestock – it's true.

EURYBATES
I have a few sheep myself at home, and a couple of goats.

CIRCE
Fascinating.

EURYBATES
And a pig. An old grunter. Mind you, he'll be bacon
by now.

CIRCE
Won't you take off your cloak and be seated, Captain?

POLITES
I saw . . . I just thought I . . . is that a wolf in the garden?

CIRCE
She-wolf. Female. But that's a male. See him – curled
under the magnolia tree. He's a beauty, isn't he?

POLITES
That's . . . a lion.

CIRCE
Captain, you do know your natural history.

POLITES
Aren't they . . . aggressive?

[120]

CIRCE

On the contrary. They're my puppies. My kittens.
There's no violence here. Give me your hand –

She places his hand over her heart.

Can't you feel the calmness, the peace, the delight . . .

POLITES (*seduced*)

Forgive me. It's been such a long time.

CIRCE

Here, drink all of this, before your men empty the cellar.

He downs a full glass of the wine-potion.

POLITES

Absolute nectar. Thank you.

CIRCE (*to Eurybates*)

So you were saying you kept animals of the porcine
variety.

EURYBATES

Say what?

ELPENOS

She's asking if you keep pigs.

EURYBATES

Oh, right. Just the one. A big porker he was, with a
SQUOINK! Oh, pardon my manners, ma'am. Must be
the wine. Haven't tasted such SQUOINK! SQUOINK!

ELPENOS

You can't hold your drink – you're an embarrassment.
Do ignore him, he's such a pig. Not fit to go GROINK!
GROINK! GROINK!

EURYBATES

Are you taking the SQUOINK! SQUOINK! Don't laugh
at me – you've got a snout instead of a SQUOINK!
SQUOINK! SQUOINK! SQUOINK!

ELPENOS

Think that's funny? You've – GROINK! GROINK!
GROINK! – got a tail growing out of your GROINK!
GROINK!

EURYBATES

SQUOINK! GROINK! Hey, what's – GRUNK!
GRUNK! – going on?

ELPENOS

GRRRRRRRUUUUUOOOOIIIIIINNNNNK! Help!
Captain!

CIRCE

Oh, he's got problems of his own. He can't help you, can
you, Captain?

POLITES

SSQQQQQQQQQUUUUUUUUUUEEEEEEEEAAAA . . .

*

Eurylochus bursts through the woods onto the beach.

EURYLOCHUS

Odysseus, help. We're bewitched.

ODYSSEUS

Catch your breath. Say what's happened.

EURYLOCHUS

Evil magic and dark mystery. A woman singing –

an exquisite voice, I felt my heart melting.
She invited them in for supper and drink.
I watched through the window. Odysseus,
she's beautiful, breathtaking. Suddenly
one of the men put down his goblet of wine
and there on the front of his face was a . . .

ODYSSEUS

A what?

EURYLOCHUS

A snout –
not a nose but a snout, and out of his mouth
fell a long, rough, disgusting, lolloping tongue . . .

SHIPMATE

Sounds like he's been at the drink himself!

EURYLOCHUS

NO – I sensed a trap and waited outside.
Not one drop of intoxicant has passed my lips.

ODYSSEUS

I'm afraid I believe you. Tell us what else.

EURYLOCHUS

Another man reached forward for a piece of fruit
and . . . and out popped a pink curly tail from the base
of his spine. And there at the end of his cuffs,
instead of hands – two dirty big hooves.
But Odysseus, she's beautiful, so beautiful . . .

ODYSSEUS

This could only be the woman they call Circe.
It's her magic they've fallen for. And what of Polites –
is he spellbound as well? Did he drink the brew?

EURYLOCHUS

He dropped to the floor with the rest,
snuffled among the crumbs on all fours
while the witch herded them outside into a sty,
laughing madly at her wicked trick.
Where he once had a handsome face
he now has jowls and two white tusks.

ODYSSEUS

It's Circe's work – no question. I should have guessed.
I should have gone myself in the first place.
Which direction is the palace? I'll have to find a way
to unwork this magic of hers before it sticks.

EURYLOCHUS

Head for the heart of the island if you must.
The gardens and grounds crawl with wild beasts –
lions and wolves – but they nuzzle at your hands,
roll over at your feet. They're doped.
There's dark practice at work in that manor.
But she's so beautiful, so beautiful . . .

ODYSSEUS

Guard the ship.
And if a tiger or bear or wild boar
comes crashing onto the beach later today,
don't cut out its heart for sacrifice, or light a fire
and dish it out as meat – it might be me.

*

*On his way to Circe's palace, Odysseus senses a presence
near by.*

ODYSSEUS

Who is it? Don't hide in the bushes, coward,
step onto the path and make yourself known.

HERMES

You'll know me soon enough, and then you'll give
thanks.

ODYSSEUS

Come out of the undergrowth, or I'll hack into it.

HERMES

You'd wave your sword at a God, Odysseus?

ODYSSEUS

God? What God? You're a servant of the witch.

HERMES

I serve only Zeus. Cast your eyes over me, Odysseus.
Who has wings at his feet and carries a golden staff?

ODYSSEUS

Only the God Hermes.

HERMES

Then look at the God Hermes.

ODYSSEUS

I . . . why would a God meet Odysseus on such a lonely
path?

HERMES

Hermes – the God of travellers, guide in the wilderness –
where else should you meet him but such a place?
Now look again at him and listen to his voice.

Your friends are held behind a gate in Circe's pens –
transformed into pigs. You rush towards them

hoping to set them free, but do exactly as I say,
word for word, or you'll suffer the same fate.

ODYSSEUS

Forgive my ignorance, Hermes. I put away my sword.

HERMES

Do that. It isn't a weapon you need but a plant.

ODYSSEUS

To offer to Circe? To flatter her with, or to trade?

HERMES

To keep to yourself. She'll hand you a slug of wine –
drink it back. It's the same potion that turned your men
to swine. Drink it down – right to the last drop.

ODYSSEUS

Then what? Wait for hooves to appear at my wrists?

HERMES

There's a rare flower that grows here in the grass.
The moly. Track it down and pluck it from its bed.
You'll know it when you see it. The stem is black,
and its black roots have a tight grip on the earth.
But its petals are white. Vibrant, incandescent white.

In your possession that flower will keep you safe.
You'll be inoculated, resistant to the drug
and any other devilment or spell she throws your way.

Repel her. Then draw your sword, and she'll do as you say.

ODYSSEUS

Show me where this moly flower grows.

HERMES

I'm not here to lead you by the nose, Odysseus,

only to whisper a word or two of advice.
Find it yourself. Grub it out. Remember, black
at the root and stem, petals incandescent white.

Black at the root and stem, petals incandescent white . . .

*

Odysseus enters Circe's palace later.

CIRCE

And here's the handsomest warrior of them all.

ODYSSEUS

Where are my men?

CIRCE

Having fun. You're very tense, here in the shoulders
and the neck. Why don't you relax?

ODYSSEUS

I've come for my men.

CIRCE

Are you sure? Are you sure it isn't a woman you're
looking for?

ODYSSEUS

We're sorry to have disturbed you.
We're just passing through, looking for supplies.

CIRCE

Then help yourself to whatever you see.
Doesn't this delicious-looking food tempt you?

ODYSSEUS

I'll only eat when the rest of the crew can be fed.

CIRCE

Then a drink. Who would begrudge you a drink?
Here, the sweetest wine ever to touch your lips.
Taste it. Let it loose on your tongue.
Let it loose in your blood.

Odysseus drains the glass.

Ha! You're a thirsty swine. Now get to the sty with the
rest of the litter.

ODYSSEUS

I think not. I won't be eating from any trough, Circe.

CIRCE

What! You'll not resist me.
Be a pig, I say. Be a pig.

ODYSSEUS

I hear no squealing or grunts.

CIRCE

BE A PIG. BE A PIG.

ODYSSEUS

I feel no long floppy ears. I see no sprouting tail.

CIRCE (*She beats his chest.*)
PIG, PIG. PIG, PIG.

ODYSSEUS (*He grabs her by the neck, half-choking her, and
draws his sword*).
What sort of hog could handle a weapon, like this pig
can?
Rest the blade – just so – on the butcher's neck?
What name will you give to this beast?

CIRCE

You . . . you're Odysseus. Here in my house!
Hermes predicted you'd come one day,
with your twisting words like a box of snakes.

With your . . . iron strength, your quick tongue, your
golden face . . .

ODYSSEUS

And how accurate he was. How truthful and precise.

CIRCE (*suddenly passionate*)

Odysseus, I can't tell you how long I've brooded on this.
Other men turn to low, pathetic creatures in my eyes,
but you resist, you resist. Come to my bed, Odysseus . . .

ODYSSEUS

One minute she's sending me to the farmyard,
the next she's pulling me under the sheets . . .

CIRCE

We'll make magical love, Odysseus.
We'll bring our powers together, pool our strength.
Mix with me, Odysseus. Let your limbs tangle with mine,
let your thoughts become mine.
(*whispers*)
You'll fuck me, Odysseus . . .

ODYSSEUS

You'll show me some courtesy, Circe.

I'll eat and drink with you, take
some of the delicacies you offer.
What hungry man could resist such a feast?

But first, unlock my men from the pens,
and wave your wand over their heads.

Then swear you'll keep your magic to yourself,
and swear you'll help us in our journey home.

CIRCE
I do, I do.   .

ODYSSEUS
Once every ounce of rind on their backs
is restored to flesh, and they stand upright
and speak with a human voice, then I'll taste
a little of what you spread in front of me.
But first swear. Swear on your life.

CIRCE
I promise, Odysseus. I swear.

IN THE PALACE OF THE PHAEACIANS

ALCINOUS

And did they regain their human form?

ODYSSEUS

They did. And then they washed,
scrubbed till their skin was raw,
trying to scour away the smell of pig,
spitting the taste of pig from their throats,
coughing pig out of their lungs.

ARETE

And the herb went on keeping you from harm?

ODYSSEUS

Its powers went deeper than any witch's spell.

NAUSICAA

And afterwards I presume you told that scheming,
conniving hostess of yours to go to Hades on a horse and
    cart?
Or even lopped off her head with your sword?

ODYSSEUS

No, it was . . . I judged it more complicated than that.
The men were in need of rest and shelter.

NAUSICAA

How could you stay, even for another hour?

ODYSSEUS

It took upwards of a week to stitch the sail . . .

NAUSICAA

You loitered there for a week?

ODYSSEUS

    And while the boat was beached we took the chance
    to smoke the sea-worms out of the hull, re-caulk the
       prow,
    bolster the keel – that took a month . . .

NAUSICAA

    You'll be saying next you waited a full season
    for the weather to change . . .

ODYSSEUS

    In fact before we knew it a year had slipped by . . .

NAUSICAA

    A year! You must have dined many times at her table,
      Odysseus.
    You must have been one satisfied guest!

ARETE

    Finally my daughter sees the other side of him!

ODYSSEUS

    Circe restored our spirits.

NAUSICAA

    I don't doubt it for a minute.

ARETE

    We're women. We know what this smacks of.

ODYSSEUS

    I can see where that line of thought might lead.
    But I had to consider the men:
    when we landed they were bone-weary
    and half-drowned. Their eyes carried no light.
    Months at sea had turned their fingers to rope
    and their brains to salt. Whenever they spoke

it was only to curse or to plot mutiny.
They needed fattening up and thawing out.
They needed to rest. It took twelve long months.

LEAVING *ACHAEA*

A year has passed since Odysseus and his men first arrived.

CIRCE
  I know what you're going to say.

ODYSSEUS
  My men plead with me night and day. They long for
    home.

CIRCE
  Then they can go.
  But you could stay, Odysseus. You could live with me
    here.

ODYSSEUS
  I could. But my heart begs me to leave.

CIRCE
  Think of the times we've had.
  We've bathed in the sacred streams.
  Lazed in the afternoons on cushions of purple silk.
  Eaten from silver plates.
  Sipped wine from gold cups.

ODYSSEUS
  Circe . . .

CIRCE (*whispering*)
  We've fallen asleep together under the stars,
  woken on thick fleeces,
  taken whatever we pleased,
  wanted for nothing . . .

ODYSSEUS

With every day that passes it gets harder to leave . . .

CIRCE

Whatever you've asked for, I've given.
It's all yours, Odysseus.
Why deny what you most desire . . .

POLITES (*from afar*)

Odysseus, the wind fills the sails.
The men are waiting for orders. Odysseus?

CIRCE

Odysseus, Odysseus . . .
You've feasted on fantasy with me. You still want more.
You crave me . . .

ODYSSEUS

You whisper your magic in my ear.
You swore an oath.

CIRCE

You'll tear my heart out if you leave.
And you'll leave your own heart here with me.

ODYSSEUS

If I stay you'll have broken your word.
What will I feel about you then?

POLITES (*calling*)

Odysseus? Odysseus?

CIRCE

Go, then, if you must.
But travel first to the Land of the Dead,
speak with Tiresias. Even as a blind corpse
he has the Gift. Seek him out. Hear his advice.

ODYSSEUS

How does a living mortal enter the Land of the Dead?

CIRCLE

There's no map, only a current. An undertow.

ODYSSEUS

To the wooded coast?

CIRCE

Into the flooded forest. Do you know the journey?

ODYSSEUS

I've heard tell but never believed it.
Through the groves of Persephone?

CIRCE

Between and amongst the black poplars.
And past the trees of dying fruit.
Stinking things, heavy with rot. Beyond those.
To a shore where leaf-mould and decay
make it difficult to breathe. Anchor the boat
and walk to the spit where two rivers
curdle and merge. To one side there's a bluff,
a looming, swaying, overhanging rock . . .

Go. Cast off. I'll stand on the cliff,
watching you out of sight.
You'll feel my nails in your back,
taste the blood of my last kiss.

ODYSSEUS

This way, under the crag. This is the way she described.
Eurylochus and Polites, accompany me.

EURYLOCHUS

If the dead come here, then may the Gods keep me alive.
The agony and humiliation of old age has nothing on this.
I'll hold my dying breath, I'll cling to life by my
    fingernails.

POLITES

The air reeks. The breeze carries a sour breath.

ODYSSEUS

Here in the river sand, help me dig a pit, just as Circe
    said.
About an elbow's length in each direction and a span
    deep.

EURYLOCHUS

I'll chop out the gravel with my sword and rake it aside.

ODYSSEUS

Polites, did you bring the libations?

POLITES

I have them here.

ODYSSEUS

Pass them in order, as she instructed.

*Speaking into the void, he pours each liquid into the pit in
turn.*

Here's drink for the dead. Succulent honey blended with
  milk.
And here's drink for the dead. Sweet wine from the pick
  of the vines.
And here's drink for the dead. Pure water from the
  mountain stream.

EURYLOCHUS
And now the grain, Odysseus.

ODYSSEUS
And here's the seed of the field, a scatter of barley.

And on my return to Ithaca, I swear to slaughter
the prime bull of the herd in the name of the dead,
and light a bonfire of treasure to you, Tiresias.

POLITES
See how the liquid bubbles and stews.

ODYSSEUS
Now the blood.

EURYLOCHUS
You men, bring the sheep.

*The men manhandle the scuffling and bleating sheep towards
the pit.*

The ram first. Hold it firm on its side – there, at the pit.
I'll bare its throat for your sword, Odysseus.

ODYSSEUS *(calling into the void again)*
And here's rich, dark blood for the dead.

*He draws his sword and cuts the animal's throat. Blood
spurts and pours into the pit.*

EURYLOCHUS

    Now the black ewe. Don't fight it, Polites.
    Don't break its neck before the blade takes its life.
    Ready, Odysseus.

ODYSSEUS (*to the ghosts*)

    Rouse yourselves. Come gather round this purple pool
    which overflows in your name. Be drawn to the blood.

*The blood of the black ewe gushes into the pit. The
harrowing wails and moans of the dead start up in the
distance, coming nearer.*

    Look – now they flock to me, the dead.
    Up out of Hades they come,
    the souls of the departed.
    Unhappy crowd, sorrowful mob.
    Young brides, unmarried boys,
    babes who died in the cot,
    old men who perished alone,
    women with their hearts weeping,
    battalions of men who died at war,
    some still in their battledress,
    some still with their shields raised.
    Look how they swarm
    like bats from a cave.
    See how this puddle of blood
    attracts them from the grave.
    Pitiful, pitiful the massed ranks
    of the lost, restless in death.
    A million troubled, weightless ghosts.

EURYLOCHUS (*frightened*)

    Keep them at bay with your sword.
    Swish it through the air.

POLITES

No, dip the sword in the blood
and call out Tiresias by name.

ODYSSEUS (*He dips his sword in the blood-filled pit, and
calls out.*)
I offer blood on my blade.
Tiresias – I offer blood on my blade.

TIRESIAS

Who disturbs Tiresias?
Who stirs him from his sleep?

ODYSSEUS

I . . . Odysseus.

TIRESIAS

Odysseus, is it? Come to pick my brains.

ODYSSEUS

Here's fresh blood. Drink as much as you please.

TIRESIAS

Cruel and cunning, Odysseus. No ghost
can resist the taste of liquid flesh.
No soul can refuse communion with the living wine.
(*He laps at the blood.*)
Still warm. Still warm.

ODYSSEUS

One question, Tiresias – will I ever reach home?

TIRESIAS

Ha! That's what brings you here, is it . . .
slumming it with the bone brigade . . .
I'll tell you this much . . . Poseidon won't rest.

You burnt out his son's eye – now he's hell-bent on
    revenge.
But will you reach home? You might . . .
Can you restrain the crude desires of your men? – that's
    the question.
Can you restrain your own?
(*entering a vision-state*)
I see . . . the Island of Thrinacia . . .
I see the Sun God, Helios – his herd – the Cattle of the
    Sun –
prime, graceful, docile
– their limbs thick with beef.
Swallow your appetite . . . leave them to graze.
Leave that slow, lumbering herd in peace,
and you might see Ithaca again.
But harm them in any way . . . I see broken ships . . .
    broken friends . . .
I see your house, Odysseus, your wife Penelope
besieged by coarse, rapacious men
. . . a house of suffering . . . I see . . . I see . . . the vision
    fades.

POLITES
    But another comes forward – a woman. Who is it?

EURYLOCHUS
    I can't tell – it's nothing more than a shade.

ODYSSEUS
    Come forward. Approach the blood.

POLITES
    Oh, the Gods help poor Odysseus. I know that shape.

EURYLOCHUS
    Oh, you poor, bedevilled man. My poor, tortured king.

ODYSSEUS

Is it . . .
Is it . . .
. . . mother . . .?

ANTICLEIA

Oh, my beautiful boy, still alive.

ODYSSEUS

Mother, why are you here with these shabby ghosts?
These phantoms are no company for your living heart.

ANTICLEIA

Not living, Odysseus. This heart has stopped.

ODYSSEUS (*grief-stricken*)

No . . . No . . .

ANTICLEIA

There's no pulse, now. No strength
to take my beautiful boy in my arms.

ODYSSEUS

But I left you happy and well.
(*angry*)
Who tricked you into this long sleep?
Who shall I hunt down in revenge?
Who'll pray to highest heaven that he never lived?

ANTICLEIA

Not murder, Odysseus. Not foul play.

ODYSSEUS

Then how? You were too young in years
to just close your eyes and die.

ANTICLEIA

I died of grief for my son.
For you, Odysseus. I died for you.

Once a woman bears a child
her heart's no longer her own.
When that child is lost,
so is the will to go on.
Grief for the missing is worse
than grief for the dead.

I died of longing, Odysseus.
I died of my love for you.

And your wife, Penelope – she waits.
She waits in Ithaca – dying the same death.

ODYSSEUS

No! This is an optical trick.
The Gods have twisted me one way, then another;
they're out to deceive me – this is their latest illusion.

ANTICLEIA

No, my Odysseus, what you see is truth.
This is what happens once death has made its choice.

The blood drains. The nerves become numb.
Flesh won't cling to the scaffold of bones.

The heat of life cools to a powdery ash.
The bird of the soul flies from its branch.

(*Her voice begins to fade.*)
Leave, now. Find the daylight that feeds you.
Fight your way home to your wife.

ODYSSEUS (*calling into the darkness, sobbing*)
    Mother, mother . . .

Odysseus falls to his knees in tears.

POLITES
    Oh, beleaguered man. Sorrowful king. My heart weeps.

EURYLOCHUS
    And here come other familiar faces.
    Old comrades. Brothers in arms from Troy.

ODYSSEUS
    Agamemnon? Agamemnon?

AGAMEMNON
    Odysseus. Once we fought shoulder to shoulder.
    Now I creep from the shadows to beg for blood
    at your feet.

ODYSSEUS (*bewildered and tearful*)
    Great leader. Proud and mighty soldier.

AGAMEMNON
    Death makes me a vagrant and scavenger.

ODYSSEUS
    Were you shipwrecked on the journey home?
    Or ambushed by some rogue army?

AGAMEMNON
    Nothing as proud as that.
    Not killed in battle or crushed by Poseidon's fist.

    Murdered! Worse – murdered by my wife
    and her lover. Cut down in my own house.
    While we battled for Troy, she rolled in the sheets.
    While we defended our lives, she opened her legs.

When I returned, victorious, exhausted,
succulent food was prepared. Stabbed in the back
I died face-down in the fruits and breads and meats
of my own homecoming feast.

ODYSSEUS

Disloyalty and deceit. Sick treachery.

AGAMEMNON

She brought shame on every woman and wife.
Beware of womankind, Odysseus. Not Penelope . . .
She was just a young bride when we sailed to war
with your new-born son at her breast.

POLITES

And yet another ghost. Another familiar face.

EURYLOCHUS

The vaults of death are rammed full with our friends.

ODYSSEUS

Achilles.

ACHILLES

You've wandered into the wrong territory, Odysseus.
You were always the luckiest man alive –
this is no place for the fortunate.
Everyone here has lost.

ODYSSEUS

Good Achilles, you're still my glorious nobleman,
my God-like lord.

ACHILLES

Praise is wasted here. It dies on the lips.
There are no leaders and no one to lead.
Make no mistake – this is the bitter end.

Does it appal? Does it look as bad as it feels?
Don't fall for the dream of the afterlife,
Odysseus. Live on as a maggot or worm
eating the dirt of the world or feeding on rancid meat.
Anything but this.

There's no glory in battle, no glorious death.
If I ever spoke of glorious death I take back those words.
Death and glory should never inhabit the same breath.

AGAMEMNON
But tell me of my son. Is he still alive?

ACHILLES
No, tell me about my boy first.

ODYSSEUS
Achilles, Agamemnon . . . what shall I say?

AGAMEMNON
Don't leave us in eternal doubt. Odysseus, please . . .

ACHILLES
Say something before it's too late. Cruel Odysseus.

ODYSSEUS
No, I . . .

POLITES
Look, the blood runs dry. They begin to fade.

The pleading voices of Agamemnon and Achilles fade away.

ACHILLES
Odysseus, please, please . . .

AGAMEMNON
Odysseus . . .

Odysseus is left weeping.

EURYLOCHUS
Help me lift him.

They haul him to his feet.

Lean on us, Odysseus.

Let's flee this sinister watering hole.
Who knows how many of our family and friends
have entered the grave since we saw them last?
Who knows which face might appear next from the dark?

IN THE PALACE OF THE PHAEACIANS

NAUSICAA

Phaeacians – look with wonder on this sufferer,
listen to his story. You doubted him at first,
when I found him shivering in a nest of leaves.
But his words resurrect him before our eyes.

ALCINOUS

Odysseus, we mostly look on strangers with a cold stare.
Fraudsters and tricksters have landed here,
twisting their tongues into our ears.
But you're no con man. You're too honest
and open-hearted to be anything but true.
I believe even my wife . . . Arete?

ARETE (*disturbed and moved*)

The part with the mother . . .
The mother dying of grief for her child . . .
Meeting the mother beyond the grave . . . I found . . .
I couldn't bear . . .

NAUSICAA

You have the voice of a singer, Odysseus,
and a poet's charm for bringing the past to life.
We could listen all day and all night.

ODYSSEUS

Then let me, in honour of my brave men,
describe the final chapters of their lives.
Men who fought and won the battle for Troy
only to founder and fall on the journey home.

THE SIRENS

ODYSSEUS
Rest the oars for a moment while I talk.

POLITES (*shouts*)
Men, rest the oars.

ELPENOS (*under his breath*)
Here comes one of those big speeches.

ODYSSEUS
We're not drifting aimlessly, as some of you think.
We have a direction and a destination, and we're on
    course.
We didn't visit the Land of the Dead for no reason
but to take our bearings from the mouth of Tiresias.

ELPENOS (*whispering*)
Great, now we're getting instructions from a blind man.

EURYBATES
Yeah, and a dead one at that.

ODYSSEUS
We're bound for Thrinacia. It's a landmark.
And after that, it's only three or four short hops
from island to island before we reach our home,
our Ithaca.
But it's a hazardous route . . .

Groans from the crew.

Listen to me. Listen to what Tiresias said.
Your lives and my life are intertwined.
There's no unravelling the knot. Your lives

depend on mine – that's what this tangle means.
You'd do well to remember that. Bring me
a bowl of beeswax. We sail for Thrinacia.

ELPENOS
What did he ask for?

EURYBATES
Beeswax.

ELPENOS
What does he want beeswax for?

EURYBATES
Don't ask me. Maybe he's going to get down on his hands
and knees and polish the deck.

ELPENOS
Maybe he's lost the plot.

                                    *

*They have sailed on for an hour or so when the wind begins
to drop.*

EURYBATES
Hey, feel that?

ELPENOS
What?

EURYBATES
The breeze.

ELPENOS
There isn't any. It's gone still.

EURYBATES

That's right. That's what I mean.

POLITES

Odysseus? Odysseus?

ODYSSEUS

Has the sail gone limp?

POLITES

Hanging like a veil. There isn't a breath of air.

ODYSSEUS

Assemble the crew.

A faint singing begins in the faraway distance, then fades.

There isn't much time.

POLITES (*shouts*)

Everyone in line, double quick.

The men assemble on deck.

ODYSSEUS

Men, we're making good headway,
but the Island of the Sirens looms.

On pain of death, don't let their songs
enter your head. Here's beeswax for your ears –
I've kneaded it all afternoon in the sun.
Here, every one of you, take a gobbet,
and when I give the signal
bung it deep in your lugs. Good.

Now get the strongest rope on board
and lash me tightly to the mast . . .
Bind me in coils of rope.

POLITES
Sir, we wouldn't dream of roping you like a wild horse . . .

ODYSSEUS
And then row and row and row.
Dig into the waves as if you were drunk
and digging for gold. No – tunnelling
out of a grave. As if you were buried alive.
And whatever I say, however much I scream
or threaten or plead – ignore every word.

Is that clear?

So do it. NOW.

They lash him to the mast

ODYSSEUS
Now bung your ears with the wax, and row for your lives.

*A silence descends. The noise of the men and the sound of
the waves gradually disappear. The song of the Sirens enters
Odysseus' head.*

SIRENS
Here where the fires burn . . .
Here where the stars glow . . .
Here where the fruits grow . . .
Here where the heart turns . . .
    Come, Odysseus. Odysseus, come . . .

ODYSSEUS (*moaning*)
This is witchery . . . but pleasant. Soothing.

SIRENS
Here where the fires glow . . .
Here where the stars turn . . .

> *Here where the fruits burn . . .*
> *Here where the heart grows . . .*
>> *Come, Odysseus. Odysseus, come . . .*

ODYSSEUS

> This music touches me. It has fingers and hands.
> I feel its breath. I feel its mouth. Oh . . .

SIRENS

> *Here where the fires turn . . .*
> *Here where the stars grow . . .*
> *Here where the fruits glow . . .*
> *Here where the heart burns . . .*
>> *Come, Odysseus. Odysseus, come . . .*

ODYSSEUS

> Men, put down your work and untie me.
> Listen, listen to the pull of it, the pull of it . . .

SIRENS

> *Here where the fires grow . . .*

ODYSSEUS

> . . . fires grow . . .

SIRENS

> *Here where the stars burn . . .*
> *Here where the fruits turn . . .*

ODYSSEUS

> . . . where the . . . where the . . .

SIRENS

> *Here where the heart glows . . .*

ODYSSEUS

> . . . where the heart glows . . .

SIRENS AND ODYSSEUS
Come, Odysseus. Odysseus, come . . .

ODYSSEUS
Sail nearer to the shore – that's an order.
Men, angels are calling us – don't ignore them.
All my treasures are yours if you take me closer.
Untie me, I'll stab any man who disobeys me.
Eurylochus, friend, slit these ropes with a blade.
Men – a woman for every one of us – they promise us.
Polites, I command you to sail towards that chorus.
Untie me now. Now. Untie me, you bastard scum.
Zeus, hear me. I'll sacrifice everything in your name.
All my flocks and herds, all my land and estates . . .
All my servants and slaves . . . these men . . . take
    them . . .
(*desperate*)
My son, Telemachus . . . my wife, Penelope . . .
(*sobbing*)
Take them all, but guide me into these voices . . .
Zeus, kill me afterwards, but show me their faces . . .

I CAN'T LIVE WITHOUT KISSING THE MOUTHS
OF THE SIRENS.

*He wails and moans as the ship passes the island and the
music dies away in the distance.*

SCYLLA AND CHARYBDIS

Later. Odysseus comes to with the men standing around him.

ODYSSEUS

Is it over?

POLITES

Some time ago. You passed out.

ODYSSEUS

The singing, what if it starts up . . .

EURYLOCHUS

We're out of earshot. We thought it safe to untie you.

ODYSSEUS

Eurylochus, and you, my faithful Polites.
Wild thoughts came into my mind,
loose words came out of my mouth . . .

EURYLOCHUS

We couldn't hear you.

POLITES

Beeswax – remember.

ODYSSEUS

Then let the Gods forgive me,
for they surely heard.

POLITES

But why did you put yourself through it?
You could have plugged your ears like the rest of us.

EURYLOCHUS
He's the only man to have heard the sirens and lived.
Isn't that right, Odysseus? One more claim to fame.

POLITES
It's all in the past now.
Let's pray for plain sailing.

An almighty burst of thunder booms across the ocean.

SHIPMATE
Look out, rocks up ahead.

EURYLOCHUS
What is it – a reef of some kind?

SHIPMATE
Some form of narrow channel between two islands.

POLITES
A crag on one side and a cliff on the other.
Do we sail through it, Odysseus? What's the order?

ODYSSEUS
Achaeans – clench your hearts into fists.
We've lived through danger time and time again.

EURYLOCHUS
A trench of fuming water – it that our passageway?

ODYSSEUS
Don't feel small and weary, men.
Feel battle-hardened – toughened and tempered
by the heat of skirmish and war.

POLITES
And the wind – it's dropped to a dead calm. Should we
turn about?

ODYSSEUS

There'll be no doubling back –
the way home lies straight ahead.
Oarsmen, strike the waves
with a strong, quiet beat and don't flinch.
Don't lift your heads until we're through.

EURYLOCHUS

What do you know that we don't?

ODYSSEUS

Two perils.
On the port side – a whirlpool. Charybdis!
Three times a day she opens her throat
and swallows the sea, sucks all and sundry
into a burning, sulphurous pit. Enter that vortex
and we'll never see the light of day again.
No wooden craft could survive her gullet.
Ships that have used the trailing fig tree
on the rocky crag as a marker or flag
have been dragged down into her guts.
She vomits the bones of sea-dragons and whales.

POLITES

Then we'll steer clear.

EURYLOCHUS

Tilt the rudder. Men, make for the starboard cliff.

ODYSSEUS

No – on that side there's a greater evil.
See the mouth of that cave, draped in mist.
Six-headed Scylla sleeps in its depth.
A writhing mass of limbs, she reeks of death.
Each neck of hers is a tentacle, each of her heads

a killing machine – three racks of teeth to every jaw.
Wake her, and we'll be mince in her mouth.

EURYLOCHUS
So we're done for.

ODYSSEUS
Not if we hold our nerve.
Oarsmen – keep on with that muffled stroke.
A swift, straight course and we'll cheat both these perils.
Be metal-headed and iron-hearted, men.
Don't swerve from the task.

SHIPMATE
Sir, something stirs in the cave.

ODYSSEUS
Hold your course.

SHIPMATE
It's heard us. Look, there in the mist. It's . . . hideous.

ODYSSEUS
Hold your course.

POLITES
Steer the other way.

EURYLOCHUS
No, not to this side.
A black hole opens up – look – a steaming abyss –
the sea pours into it.
Keep away from the brink.
Pull to the other side.

ODYSSEUS
Oarsmen – harder now, and faster.

SHIPMATE

We're trapped. We've sailed into the mouth of death.

ODYSSEUS

Hold your course.

POLITES

The monster. She's looming over the cliff, waiting to pick
us off.
Do something, Odysseus.

ODYSSEUS

Row harder and straighter. Heads down. Eyes forward.

EURYLOCHUS

Keep to starboard – we're being sucked in.

SHIPMATE

I can smell her breath. Heave to port. No . . . Here she
comes.

POLITES

Load up with arrows and spears – fire at will.

ODYSSEUS

Don't inflame her. Hold your course, I say.

POLITES

We won't die without a fight. Let fly, men, let fly.

Arrows are loosed off, spears fly through the air.

SHIPMATE

They bounce off her flesh. Now she's on the rampage.

EURYLOCHUS

Heave away – we're too close to the edge.

SHIPMATE
No . . . No . . . Save us. Save us.

The men scream as Scylla's six heads whip through the air,
snatching oarsmen out of the boat.

POLITES
We're defenceless.

SHIPMATE
Six men plucked from their seats.

POLITES
She slithers back to her cave, one in each mouth.

SHIPMATE
We'll never see them again.
They're hers for life now – hopeless prisoners.

POLITES
No – it's more savage than that.
Look, she gorges on them. Gulps them down.
Hammer the waves before she comes back for more.

SHIPMATE
Row – row – we'll be eaten alive.

EURYLOCHUS
Harder and faster – I think we're pulling clear.

Behind them, the six stricken men call out Odysseus' name
until their final breath.

ODYSSEUS *(forlornly)*
Hold your course. Heads down. Eyes forward. Hold your
course.

THRINACIA

ODYSSEUS

And we praise those friends who are now lost.

MEN

Praise them.

ODYSSEUS

We salute their bravery and courage.

MEN

Salute them.

ODYSSEUS

We honour their families – those who are born of them,
those they were born from.

MEN

Honour them.

ODYSSEUS

And in their absence we grieve, and in grief
remember them.

MEN

Remember them.

ODYSSEUS

Raise the marker stone in their name
and sound the horn.

One long, steady note is blown softly from a conch.

ODYSSEUS

Let their souls rest. Let their troubles sleep.
(*changing tone*)

Men, we'll take refuge here for a while.
Mend the boat and tend to your wounds.
We're on the last leg, now. We're closing in on Ithaca.
It's time to start dreaming of home
and not be frightened of waking up.
It's within our grasp and it's real.
You're heroes – all of you – for making it this far.

But don't get too comfortable here.
Don't stray from the beach. Don't take what isn't yours.

EURYLOCHUS

What do you mean?

ODYSSEUS

Just keep your hands to yourself – that's all.

EURYLOCHUS

You're a hard-nosed leader, Odysseus.

ODYSSEUS

Explain that remark, Eurylochus.

EURYLOCHUS

Look at us. What a rag-and-bone army we are.
We've sailed with you for a decade now,
zig-zagging between islands, drifting on the current.
We've been mangled and battered at every turn.
Look at us. We have broken limbs, smashed bones,
ruptured organs, and our hearts . . .
our hearts are utterly bent out of shape.

ODYSSEUS

We've all suffered equally and the same.

EURYLOCHUS

But your will is greater than ours. You're superhuman.
You must be made out of stone by comparison.

ODYSSEUS

What's this back-handed compliment leading to?

EURYLOCHUS

It explains your coldness.
Look around you – this is a land of plenty.

ODYSSEUS

Don't lead the men astray with your rogue thoughts.

EURYLOCHUS

Did you ever see such bounty?
A herd of cattle grazes in fields above the coast –
swaying through meadow grass, heavy with meat.
Just one of those steers would feed us all . . .

ODYSSEUS

Leave those cattle alone.

EURYLOCHUS

But why shouldn't we eat?
We're half-starved, half-drowned, half-alive,
and you'd have us put back to sea on empty bellies.

ODYSSEUS

Close your mutinous mouth.

EURYLOCHUS

Just tell us why. Explain why we shouldn't feed.

ODYSSEUS

You know why. You were there.

EURYLOCHUS

Because Tiresias looked into his crystal ball?

ODYSSEUS

You heard what he said.

EURYLOCHUS

He'd have said anything for a taste of blood.

ODYSSEUS

No, he's a seer of the future and a speaker of the truth.

EURYLOCHUS

He was a blind old corpse. . . .

ODYSSEUS

Are you sure it isn't yourself you think of, Eurylochus?
It's you who has the taste of blood on his tongue,
the smell of fried steak in his nose . . .

EURYLOCHUS

Not true.

ODYSSEUS

. . . the texture of roast beef between his teeth.
It's you who'll say the first thing that comes into his head
for a plate of meat.

EURYLOCHUS

I'm only saying what everyone thinks . . .

ODYSSEUS

You drooling fool.
Are you Odysseus?

EURYLOCHUS

That's a nonsense question.

ODYSSEUS
ARE YOU ODYSSEUS?

EURYLOCHUS
Of course not.

ODYSSEUS
No, and never imagine it – not for a split second.
Never dream of it. It's beyond anything you could
  envisage.

Open your ears – the lot of you.
Those cows are the Cattle of the Sun.
Helios – the Sun God – they're his herd.
They never breed. They never die.
Leave them be and we'll be granted a safe passage home.
We'll follow Tiresias' prophecy to the word.
But spill one drop of their blood, pluck one bristle
from their hide, and you can kiss goodbye to Ithaca.
For ever.

This isn't advice – it's an order.
Now pack down for the night.
There's a storm brewing.

IN THE PALACE OF THE PHAEACIANS

ODYSSEUS

    That quelled them – for the time being.
    Unlike the weather. A storm twisted up from the sea,
    fanned by a wind from the south. The south wind –
    it blew for a month, never veering or letting up.
    It cornered us in the bay, kept us penned
    like sheep when the wolf howls at the gate.
    And breakers smashed against the cliff walls to all sides –
    to venture out would have been suicide.

    So we dug in, stayed put, eating the weeds
    that grew on the shore, bringing down gulls
    with crude arrows or stones, spearing the odd fish
    from the rocks, accepting whatever sea-life
    was thrown at our feet by the storm.

    My words had frightened the men.
    But fear doesn't last, and hunger
    has first call on the brain. There were rumblings.
    Murmurs. Men grumbling under their breath,
    behind their hands.

    Once the appetite starts to talk
    it's only a matter of time.

THE CATTLE OF THE SUN

A month has passed on Thrinacia. The men huddle around a fire, talking.

EURYLOCHUS

Is he asleep?

SHIPMATE

Snoring like a buffalo. A fly crawled across his face and he
    didn't move.

POLITES

I still say we should hang fire – do as he says.

EURYLOCHUS

You didn't say that on the boat – when he told you not to
    shoot.

Oh no, you picked up a bow and arrow and let fly.

POLITES

Yes, and look what happened.

EURYLOCHUS

You disobeyed him once – you can do it again.

That's the point I'm making.

POLITES

I just want to get home.

EURYLOCHUS

The same as everyone else does. Which is why it's time to
    act.

SHIPMATE

Convince us, then. We're listening.

EURYLOCHUS

Men, I don't say these things lightly.
I've worshipped Odysseus from the very beginning.
I've followed him to the end of the earth – and half-way
    back.

But now I doubt his mind.
Face facts. We're starving to death,
and roaming free not more than a mile away
are a hundred head of prime beef.

It doesn't stack up. The equation doesn't work.

POLITES

So why doesn't he let us feast?

EURYLOCHUS

Superstition and delirium.
Tiresias in the underworld – Odysseus was truly spooked.
And seeing the ghost of his mother . . .
I think at that point he gave up.

SHIPMATE

As if he's risking our lives on purpose – is that what you
    mean?

EURYLOCHUS

As if some death-wish has entered his mind.

POLITES

You don't believe that. Do you?

EURYLOCHUS

Why else would he have steered into the teeth
of that six-headed beast, or tried to tip us
into that underwater hurricane?

No, comrades, we're in charge of our own destiny now.

There are thousands of roads that lead to death,
but starvation, that's the most painful route.
Torture – every inch. A slow, lingering demise.
I'd rather die at sea, crushed by Poseidon's fist,
than sit and watch my bones poke through my shrinking
  flesh.

SHIPMATE
He's right. He's so right.

EURYLOCHUS
Polites, what do you say?

POLITES
It makes sense, the way you explain it.
But I've got a bad feeling about this.

EURYLOCHUS
Wait till you've got a decent meal inside you.
You'll feel differently then.

POLITES
I suppose.

EURYLOCHUS
There's no suppose about it.
Look – a full moon – she'll be our guide.
It's still an hour before the Sun God rises.
Round everyone up and hand out the spears.
We're going hunting.

*

The men gather at the edge of the pasture, talking in hushed tones.

EURYLOCHUS

Look at the width of the shoulders.

POLITES

And the haunches – think of the meat on those.

SHIPMATE

Yes, and look at the length of those horns.
I wouldn't want to be on the wrong end of one of those.

ELPENOS (*loudly*)

What's all the whispering about?

POLITES

We're trying to take them by surprise.
We don't want to chase them half-way over the mountain.

ELPENOS

You're kidding, aren't you? They're as soft as pudding.

SHIPMATE

A likely story.

ELPENOS

They're completely docile.

SHIPMATE

Those prongs don't look very docile.

ELPENOS

Look at him – he's seen us, but he's not fussed. Soft article.

EURYLOCHUS

Prove it. Approach one of them.

ELPENOS

I will do. There's nothing to be afraid of.

SHIPMATE

Here, take this spear.

ELPENOS

You're not listening – I don't need one. Watch.

Elpenos sets off towards the cattle.

SHIPMATE

He's either very brave or very stupid.

POLITES

They've noticed him but they're not chasing him.

SHIPMATE

What's he doing now?

POLITES

He's touching it, pulling on its horns.

SHIPMATE

Amazing – it's kneeling down for him.

ELPENOS (*his voice from afar*)

Watch this then.

SHIPMATE

What the . . . I've seen it all now.

POLITES

He's riding it!
He's climbed on its back and he's riding it like a pony.

ELPENOS (*coming closer, astride the cow*)

Yee-ha! What did I tell you?

The bullock plods towards them.

SHIPMATE

It's unbelievable. It's . . . kind of beautiful.

POLITES

What do you say, Eurylochus?

EURYLOCHUS

Yes, a miracle. Now we know Odysseus was wrong.
This was meant to happen.

ELPENOS

Here we are, fellers. It's the only way to travel.
Beats sloshing around in a boat anyhow.

SHIPMATE

He's a magnificent animal.

POLITES

Quite awesome.

ELPENOS

Go on, stroke his nose. Feed him a clump of grass. Go on,
Eurylochus – he won't bite you.

EURYLOCHUS

An ironic statement, in the circumstances.

ELPENOS

What's he talking about?

EURYLOCHUS

Slide down from that hide, Achaean.

ELPENOS

What's the problem?

EURYLOCHUS

The problem is you're sitting astride about two tons of
raw beef.

[172]

You won't want it rolling on top of you.

Zeus, we thank you for your bounteous gifts.
Forgive us our hunger. Forgive us our sins.

*He slits the creature's throat with a knife. It lets out a long,
low death moan and slumps to the ground.*

(*salivating and excited*)
Fetch buckets – don't loose the blood-soup.
Fetch a cleaver – hack it into quarters and build a fire on
    the beach.
Then slaughter another, then another, then another.
Protein – that's what we need to get home,
not hocus-pocus and mumbo-jumbo.

No human should starve while animals live.
It's unnatural. It's not how things were meant to be.

*

*An hour or so later. Meat hisses and sizzles on a spit. The
men laugh as they feast. Odysseus wakes with a start,
sweating and talking to himself.*

ODYSSEUS
Eurylochus? Polites?

What a dream. I dreamed I was staked out
under the sun, the sun scorching my skin,
singeing my hair. Staked out till I caught fire.
What does it mean?

Eurylochus? Polites?

I need to cool down. I need to wash.

He walks to the shoreline and throws water at his face.

Oh, better. Better.
But I can still smell . . . What's that taste in the air?
(*suddenly panic-stricken*)
No, in the name of everything that matters –
tell me I'm mistaken.
(*shouting*)
Eurylochus? Polites?
(*approaching the camp fire*)
Tell me I'm wrong. Tell me this is a nightmare vision.

EURYLOCHUS

Relax, Odysseus.

ODYSSEUS

You disobeyed me.

EURYLOCHUS

Eat with us.
You'll agree with our actions once you've tasted this
    silverside.

ODYSSEUS

This is sacrilegious.

POLITES

We were all of one mind, Odysseus.
We respect your wishes, but our needs as humans have to
    come first.

EURYLOCHUS

Don't grovel. Stand your ground.

POLITES

I'm just explaining . . .

EURYLOCHUS

Don't explain and don't apologize.
No man should have to justify his need to eat.
No man should have to apologize for surviving –
not even to noble Odysseus.

ODYSSEUS

Greed and gluttony – they aren't the motives of civilized
men.

EURYLOCHUS

We were starving.

ODYSSEUS

You were slavering, like a dog.
You've wrecked everything.

EURYLOCHUS

I stand by my actions. You'll never get us home –
you've lost your bearings.

EURYBATES

Look – it moved.

POLITES

What did you say?

EURYBATES

The hide from that cow – I saw it . . .

POLITES

You have a fever.

ELPENOS

No – look. I saw it too. It's starting to . . . crawl.

EURYLOCHUS

Stop scaremongering – dead flesh doesn't move.

POLITES

You're wrong. Look, Eurylochus. That skull –
its jawbone opens and shuts.

ELPENOS

The eyes in the sockets roll and blink. Argh – the meat
on my plate.

POLITES

What?

ELPENOS

It's . . . twitching. It's alive. Urgh – get it off my leg.
Get it off.

EURYBATES

It's bewitched.

POLITES

What have we done, Eurylochus?
Every bone rattles and shakes, and the carcasses
squirm.

ELPENOS

I'm going to be sick.

EURYLOCHUS

It's nothing, it's just . . . we're imagining it.

ODYSSEUS

You've no notion of the chaos you've caused.

EURYLOCHUS

We're fine. It's the richness of the meat – making us
dream.

ODYSSEUS

You've no idea what demons you've released.

SHIPMATE (*from afar*)
    Odysseus. The wind's changed.

POLITES
    What did he say?

SHIPMATE
    The wind's swung around. We should sail now, while it
        blows fair.

POLITES
    He's right. We should sail now, shouldn't we, Odysseus?

ODYSSEUS
    Burn or bury what's left of those peaceful beasts.
    Hide your shame in the sand.

ELPENOS
    I'm not touching it – it's weird.

ODYSSEUS
    You'll do as I say or you'll join it.
    Then everyone onto the boat.

EURYLOCHUS
    So the Cattle of the Sun writhe and wriggle after their
        death –
    so what? The wind changes in our favour.
    The omens are good.

ODYSSEUS
    The omens are BAD. The Gods are ANGRY.
    And the doors of revenge open smoothly and quietly –
    we're invited in, and into them we sail, their special
        guests.

EURYLOCHUS

I'm not afraid. We're no more than a few miles from
home.

ODYSSEUS

And just the small matter of eternity in between.
I should leave you here.
Eurylochus. Traitor. Slaughterman – killer of hope.

A thunderbolt splits the air.

IN THE PALACE OF THE PHAEACIANS

ODYSSEUS

No sooner do we cast off, no sooner do we
round the point, than black clouds slide over the sky,
gather over the boat like a solid black roof.
And Zeus, on behalf of the God of the Sun
whose precious cattle were cleaved apart,
triggered thunderbolt after thunderbolt.

It didn't take long. The end was quick. The mast
snapped like a twig. The hull fragmented,
every man was pitched into the churning swell –
I saw each face go past, gulping for breath,
reaching for a hand or rope. I saw heads
rise and sink, rise and sink, then rise no more.
Eurylochus was last, choking and thrashing,
eating the sea, breathing the sea till his lungs
were dead weights in his chest, pulling him down.

I saw every last shipmate and friend drown.

ALCINOUS

But you – you stand here before us – alive.
You lived to tell the tale.

ODYSSEUS

Lived, yes. And relive it now. As if I'm back there,
afloat in the sea with broken timbers and dead men.

I catch hold of a leather strap . . . it just comes to hand.
Why do I need it? I don't know but I
hold on. Hold on. The mast rolls past on its side . . . I
    mount it,

it throws me off . . . I scramble back on. And here's
a plank or spar . . . I lash the spar to the mast with
the strap . . . Now it's a floating cross . . . A crude raft.
  The
thump of the air . . . wind pummelling my back, landing
    punch
after punch . . . I won't let go . . . I dig my fingernails
into the wood . . . I breathe when the waves reload . . .
  Hold
my breath when they erupt . . . Then it's night
    suddenly . . .
I'm still alive. Still alive.

A current sweeps me along – a race of water, heading
    where . . .
backwards? Yes, back to the channel between rocks . . .
A cave on one side . . . on the other the water moans.
Scylla again, Charybdis again . . . Zeus – spare me – make
    it quick . . .
here comes an upswell . . . within reach – just – the limb
of a fig tree . . . I grab it . . . I'll hang on . . . The blood
    drains . . .
my arms are someone else's. Then . . . is it an hour I've . . .

is it an hour I've dangled over the vortex . . .
I'll die now. This moment I'll let go . . . Or this moment
now . . . or . . . Then an earth tremor, a quake under the
    sea . . .
All Charybdis swallows she vomits back again . . .
I let go, ride the rip curl, roll in the tidal wave . . .
and here's the puked-up remains of the raft . . .
I'll row with my hands . . . I'll row for four days, five
    days . . .

I'll row with my arms, six days, seven days, eight days,
nine days, ten . . .

Delirious and breathless, Odysseus collapses on the floor.

ARETE

Catch him, someone.

ALCINOUS

Prop him in a chair – he's losing his balance.

ODYSSEUS

No, I'm fine. Let me stand.

NAUSICAA

Nonsense – you're only half conscious.
Here's a drink, Odysseus. Not salt water now – just wine.

He drains the glass.

Someone fill the glass again.

ODYSSEUS

I'm fine, really.

ALCINOUS

All so long ago, but still so clear in your mind.

ODYSSEUS

A waking dream. A living nightmare.

And you know the rest. I fetched up on Ogygia –
Calypso's island. Seven years in her grip,
then a tortuous journey here, then . . .

Who knows, if your daughter hadn't taken pity on me,
hadn't seen through the coat of leaves,
and the lice-infested hair, and the filthy skin . . .
hadn't see the man underneath. Who knows?
Ten years at war. Ten years at sea.

ALCINOUS

Odysseus, we . . .

ARETE

No – let me.
I was hesitant and unbelieving at first.
You're a weaver of tales, Odysseus,
And you're cunning and astute –
the subject of your stories is your own cleverness.
You've more guile than a million monkeys, I suspect.

But there's no doubting your desire and intent.
Your wife, your son, and your home –
they're your magnetic north.
Only a man with a passion and love like yours could have
    survived.

There's no greater cause.
Now I want nothing more than to see your journey
    complete.

ALCINOUS

Believe me, Odysseus. When Queen Arete
changes her mind, mountains have moved.
Load a ship with treasure – gifts for our new friend –
and sail him home at once.

NAUSICAA

Must he leave now?

ARETE

Yes, he must.

NAUSICAA

But have him stay another week to gather his strength . . .

ARETE

Haven't you been listening?
Every step of the way something has tripped him up.
Opportunities have been traps.
Open doors have been prisons.
Invitations have been life sentences.

People have bedevilled him – not all of them men!

He won't be sidetracked again.
We won't offer the same temptation.

NAUSICAA

No, mother.

ODYSSEUS

So compassionate.
So . . . understanding.

ALCINOUS

Believe in us – we'll see you safe home.
We have the knack of these waters –
nothing will drive you back or knock you off course.

Is a boat prepared?

SERVANT

Ready and waiting.

ALCINOUS

With gifts on board?

SERVANT

Stacked to the limit, my lord.

ALCINOUS

What crew?

SERVANT

The best oarsmen from your fleet.

ODYSSEUS

My noble lord. Merciful queen. Gracious princess.

ALCINOUS

A toast. To Ithaca's returning King. To Odysseus.

ALL

TO ODYSSEUS.

HOMEWARD BOUND

SAILOR

The sun rising just as we near land. Perfect timing.

SKIPPER

And look – the morning star – a good sign.

SAILOR

Do you know this coast?

SKIPPER

I came here fishing once.

SAILOR

Where's the best place to land?

SKIPPER

Right here, pretty much, between these jutting
promontories.
The ocean bed runs smoothly right up to the beach.
It's a natural harbour.

SAILOR

Will he be safe here?

SKIPPER

He's the king, isn't he? This is his land. Why should he
fear?

SAILOR

Kings don't usually come home by the back door.
He might be mistaken for a spy or pirate and strung up.

SKIPPER

It's not our job to worry about these things.

Here we go. Punt on till we scrape the bottom,
then everyone out and drag it up the beach.

They haul the boat into the sand.

SKIPPER
OK. Well done. Where is he?

SAILOR
Asleep, look. Under this canvas.

SKIPPER
Don't wake him, then. You others, pile the treasure
out of reach of the sea.

SAILOR
Twenty years away from home – I wanted to see his face.

SKIPPER
No, let him rest.

SAILOR
What's the longest you've ever been away for?

SKIPPER
Twelve weeks. Felt like for ever.

SAILOR
So what must this be like?
I bet even his own dog won't remember him.

SKIPPER
I can't think that a man like this will have been forgotten.

SAILOR
The world turns. Fashions change. People move on.

SKIPPER

Some things are worth waiting for.

SAILOR

No one would wait that long for me.

SKIPPER

We'll bear him on this pallet
and set him down on the beach.

They lift Odysseus from the boat and leave him sleeping on the shore.

SAILOR

Sure we shouldn't wake him?

SKIPPER

No. This seems right.
Throw the canvas back over his shoulders.

SAILOR

It'll be like waking up from a coma.
Like coming back from the dead.

SKIPPER

All unloaded?
One big shove then to cast off.

Good luck, tired Odysseus. Sleeping King of Ithaca.
Welcome home.

III

IN THE PALACE OF ODYSSEUS

The suitors are gambling and feasting.

EURYMACHUS
You bet three. I bet five, and another five.

AMPHINOMUS
That's thirteen.

EURYMACHUS
You're a mathematical genius!
Hey – more wine over here. And more meat.

AMPHINOMUS
Takes the fun out of it, doesn't it?

EURYMACHUS
The fun out of what?

AMPHINOMUS
Gambling. We drink like princes and we eat like kings.
Whatever we shout for arrives on a silver plate.
I've put on weight.

EURYMACHUS
I never get tired of winning or sick of losing.
Now lay your money down and roll the stones.

They roll the pebbles across the table.

Ha! Pay up. You're a born loser, Amphinomus,
I don't know why I hang about with you – it might rub
    off.

AMPHINOMUS
You've done all right by me.

EURYMACHUS

True – it keeps my purse fat. But look, there goes the biggest prize.

AMPHINOMUS

Where?

The hall goes quiet as the suitors register Penelope's presence.

EURYMACHUS

On the balcony – same time every night.
(*shouts*)
My sovereign lady. Won't you join us for a drink?

Or a bite to eat?

There's more than enough. Look at this plump game bird, freshly roasted. Won't you share a leg with me, my lady?

Or a breast? Will you share a breast?

AMPHINOMUS

Leave her alone.

EURYMACHUS

Shall we prise open the wishbone together, my lady?
Part it wide and make a wish.

Laughter in the hall.

AMPHINOMUS

You're deplorable.

EURYMACHUS

What's rattled your cage?

AMPHINOMUS

I just think we should show her some respect.
Vulgarity – it's hardly the way to her heart.

EURYMACHUS

And how much respect has she showed us,
stringing us along all these years? She's the vulgar one.

AMPHINOMUS

It's not what I call courtship.

EURYMACHUS

She's in no position to pick and choose.
She's a widow in all but name, and before long
she'll be penniless, and those looks won't last for ever.
Pretty soon she'll be happy to marry a goat-herd.
So stop flapping. We're in the box seat.

AMPHINOMUS

If Odysseus ever comes back . . .

EURYMACHUS

Well, he isn't coming back, so stop mithering.

Penelope leaves the balcony and a door closes behind her.

EURYMACHUS

Now look what you've done – you've scared her off.
Get your money out – we'll double the stakes.
Anyone else for a game?

Antinous strides into the hall.

ANTINOUS

Put those away.

EURYMACHUS

Hey – I'm in the middle of a winning streak.

ANTINOUS

Your luck just changed. Crowd around and listen.
News just reached me. Telemachus is back on Ithaca.

EURYMACHUS

What? We had men on the cliffs and in the bay.

ANTINOUS

He slipped past.

EURYMACHUS

How can a man slip past a hundred spears and knives?
A sea-snake couldn't have wriggled through that lot
    unscathed.

ANTINOUS

Well, he did. He was seen in the hills.

EURYMACHUS

Useless. A bunch of hopeless bunglers.
I should have done it myself.

AMPHINOMUS

This is a bad omen.

ANTINOUS

Let's keep superstition out of it. Although . . .
it's true. The fingerprints of the Gods are all over this.
Those watchmen kept guard all around the clock,
right across the bay. It was a wall of steel.
Only a God or Goddess could have spirited that boy home.

AMPHINOMUS

Not a boy any more, then.

EURYMACHUS

He's a lickspittle. A beardless wonder.

ANTINOUS

No, Amphinomus is right.
By stealing back to Ithaca he's proved what some of us
    feared –

that he's crafty and determined.
He's his father's son, in other words.
And now he's roaming the island,
turning people against us, murmuring in their ears.
We've no alternative.

AMPHINOMUS

What – murder him in cold blood?

ANTINOUS

You didn't hesitate before,
when we meant to finish him off at sea.

AMPHINOMUS

Out of sight, out of mind. But he's the heir to the
    kingdom –
we can't hunt him down in his own land.

EURYMACHUS

Kill him now.

ANTINOUS

Agreed. This thing needs bringing to a head.
Then we'll offer gifts to his mother –
she'll choose the man who makes the best offer . . .

EURYMACHUS

And we'll all live happily ever after.

AMPHINOMUS

I say we should consult the Gods – seek their judgement.

ANTINOUS

They've made their move by bringing Telemachus home.
They mean to test us – see how we respond.

We won't disappoint them.

OLYMPUS

ATHENA
Zeus? Father?

ZEUS
I'm resting.

ATHENA
It won't exhaust you to turn your head.
Look down through the clouds. What do you see?

ZEUS
Nothing. It's misty.

ATHENA
Wait a moment.
(*She blows the clouds apart.*)
Now what do you see? There, where I'm pointing.

ZEUS
An island.

ATHENA
Not just any island. Ithaca.

ZEUS
Has Athena taken to giving mighty Zeus lessons in
geography?

ATHENA
Look at that beach on the west coast.
That cove, between the two headlands.
Notice anything on the strand-line?

ZEUS

Driftwood?

ATHENA

Of a kind.

ZEUS

No, it's something alive. A large squid, is it? A dolphin?

ATHENA

It's a man.

ZEUS

Ah, and not just any man, I presume?

ATHENA

Look at the hands, the hair, the limbs beneath the clothes.
Odysseus, home after twenty years.

ZEUS

And now he sleeps like a foetus,
curled in a ball with his face buried in his chest.
Let's see if a few drops of rain might bring him round.

ATHENA

No, don't wake him.

ZEUS

Very well. The beautiful irony isn't lost on me.
The suffering hero arrives home in slumbering innocence.

ATHENA

But is he home for good, or does Poseidon
still chase him for his pound of flesh?

ZEUS

Who can say, in the great scheme of things?
Who can predict what might happen next?

Besides, your man, Odysseus –
he might be sleeping like a baby in the womb
but he rears up like a cobra when he's roused.
He blinded the Cyclops with a burning lance –
Poseidon's son! My nephew. Poseidon has a case.

ATHENA

He's your brother. Call him off.

ZEUS

I can't do that.

ATHENE

Then I'll go to Odysseus. I'll intervene.

ZEUS

Athena, not so fast.

ATHENA

He's served his time. I won't have him
clawed back into the sea by some freak wave.

ZEUS

You're being hasty – you're acting irrationally – like one
of them.

ATHENA

I'll guide him safely inland.

ZEUS

Well, if you must you must. At least go in disguise.

ATHENA

I'll appear as a shepherd boy. Goodbye, father.

ZEUS

Goodbye, goodbye, goodbye.

She's right. Poor wretch of a man –
twenty years an exile – enough is enough.
Odysseus will be spared.
But Poseidon bears his grudge like a birthright –
he'll have to be bought off.

So those Phaeacian oarsmen, who carried him
over the waves, whose craft still skims the surface
of Poseidon's watery fields . . . who can say? Who can
    say?

ON THE BEACH AT ITHACA

*A violent wave crashes in the distance as Poseidon wrecks
the Phaeacian ship. The echo of it carries across the water,
waking Odysseus from his sleep.*

ODYSSEUS
What . . . a dream . . . the end of the world . . .
No, only a storm at sea.
A freak wave cracking the keel of some poor sailing ship.
Snapping it like a twig. Just the Gods doing their thing.

He stands and dusts himself down.

How long did I sleep? Too long. And too deep –
those sweet-talking Phaeacians. The moment
I closed my eyes they dumped me on the nearest beach.

Did they take away their gifts as well,
giving to me with the right hand,
taking back with the left?
I bet they couldn't keep their fingers off this stash of loot.

He lays his hands on the riches, piled on the beach.

No, all here.
But what's the use of a golden brooch
or a ruby ring or a crown studded with precious stones
in a God-forsaken land. I'm discarded. A castaway.
I'm the king of nothing and nowhere again.
(*shouts into the air*)
I'M THE KING OF OBLIVION.

ATHENA (*disguised as a shepherd boy*)
You seem troubled, stranger. Are you lost?

ODYSSEUS (*surprised and flustered*)
Er . . . lost . . . yes. Shipwrecked. Thrown onto the beach.
Lost and a little bit delirious.

ATHENA
But the sea's been calm for weeks.

ODYSSEUS
It happened . . . some time and distance away. I drifted.

ATHENA
Lucky to be alive, then?

ODYSSEUS
Lucky beyond all imagining.
But my thoughts are in a mess – all my senses are fuddled.
The wind's whistled in my ear, the sun's warmed my
    brain
and salt water has fouled my blood.
The workings of my mind are out of kilter with the world.
I'm completely lost. I have to ask you – what island is
    this?

ATHENA
You mean you don't know?

ODYSSEUS
Hand on heart – I've no idea.

ATHENA
Then you're in worse shape than you think.

Don't you recognize this famous place,
with its rocky outcrops and jutting crags?
It's not huge, but it's rich in woodland
and birdlife, and the wells never run dry,
and crops and vines thrive in its deep soil,

and goats and cattle are fat with milk,
and herbs season the air . . .

ODYSSEUS
No, I . . .

ATHENA
Breathe its smell – doesn't it strike home?

ODYSSEUS (*breathing in*)
I must admit there's something . . .

ATHENA
Say its name. Ithaca! It's famous everywhere –
even in Troy, and that's a world away. Say it.

ODYSSEUS (*astonished*)
Ithaca?

ATHENA
Don't say you haven't heard of it.

ODYSSEUS
Ithaca. Ithaca? I . . .
(*concealing his feelings*)
I mean – yes, I've come across that name.

You see, I'm a sailor from Crete. With children
waiting for me, children with mouths to feed.
This pile of treasure, it's mainly for them.
I was sailing west when . . .

ATHENA
Odysseus – you're cunning and wily, right to the last,
some might go as far as to call you sly.
But you can stop your twisting and turning now.
You're no more a sailor from Crete than I'm a shepherd
boy.

ODYSSEUS

Who are you? What do you want?

ATHENA

Pallas Athena. Daughter of Zeus.

ODYSSEUS

My Goddess.

ATHENA

I've followed your fortunes, Odysseus.
Stood like a shield in front of you
or at your shoulder in silence.

ODYSSEUS

I've felt your presence. You've been my lucky talisman.

ATHENA

No, much more.
I've been your pole star, and your armour plating.
Without me, you wouldn't have made it this far.
You wouldn't have lived.

ODYSSEUS

I can't take it in.
I daren't let myself believe.

ATHENA

Believe it, Odysseus. You're home.

ODYSSEUS

My eyes begin to recognize the signs –
those stones . . . those plants . . . the birds . . . even the
    clouds –
all images of Ithaca – all native to this land.
But my heart won't let it be true.

ATHENA

It's as true as the ground you kneel on.
Feel the sand. Pick it up. It's Ithaca – every last grain.

ODYSSEUS (*astonished*)

Ithaca – right here in my hand.

ATHENA

Which doesn't mean your journey's over.
Hordes of suitors are camped in your house,
loving the day your wife declares herself a widow –
your death would open the bedroom doors for one of
    those hyenas.
And Penelope, who waits and waits,
you can't just go striding home after so long . . .

ODYSSEUS

I know. I need to prove myself to her.
She needs . . .
We need to prove ourselves to ourselves –
husband to wife.

ATHENA

Never impulsive. Clever like a cat.
Look, I'll bring down the mist – slip through its curtain.
Go and find Eumaeus, your old swineherd.

ODYSSEUS

What are you doing?

ATHENA

Odysseus wouldn't make it within a mile of his palace –
the suitors have their spies and their assassins.
But an old man,
with shrunken skin,
sagging limbs,

a head of silvery hair
and two dull stones in his eyes . . .

She transforms him into an old man.

ODYSSEUS
It's hardly how I imagined my return.
Tottering home, a wizened beggar.

ATHENA
There'll be no grand entrance.
Less self-consciousness and more self-preservation –
that's what's needed on this occasion.

ODYSSEUS
What about my son, Telemachus? Tell me about my son.

ATHENA
Follow the path to the right of the cliffs.
(*Her voice trails off into the distance.*)
Go now before the fog catches you in its net.

ODYSSEUS
Athena, wait . . .

A nightmare twenty years in the wilds of the world.
Then I open my eyes and I'm home. I wake from sleep,
and I'm home.

THE LOYAL SWINEHERD

*Odysseus approaches Eumaeus' farmstead. Dogs bark as he
opens the gate and nears the door.*

EUMAEUS (*from inside*)
Who's there? Who's trespassing on my land?

ODYSSEUS
A shipwrecked sailor, from Crete.
The tide washed me up on your shore.
I'm a friendly stranger. I don't mean any harm.

EUMAEUS (*opening the door*)
Friendly, eh? Oh, yes, there's no doubt about that.

ODYSSEUS (*thinking he may have been recognized*)
But you've never seen me before. How can you tell?

EUMAEUS
I can't, but these hounds can.
They've got a keen nose for that kind of thing.
They can smell danger from twenty fields away.
If you'd been a trouble-maker, old timer,
you'd be dog-meat by now.

ODYSSEUS
Then praise to all animals and their sense of right and
wrong.

EUMAEUS
I'm a farmer – I praise animals every day.
Well, come inside. It's no stately home but it's warm and
dry.

They go inside the hut.

EUMAEUS

Take the seat by the fire.

ODYSSEUS

Isn't that your seat?

EUMAEUS

Visitors have pride of place in this house.
This whole island's famous for its hospitality.
Better it wasn't – that's what I sometimes think.

ODYSSEUS

What can you mean by that?

EUMAEUS

Down at the palace.
It's crawling with spongers and layabouts,
dozens of them out-staying their welcome.
Scavengers they are. Dingoes.

ODYSSEUS

The head of the house must be a generous man.

EUMAEUS

The most generous I've ever known, and the wisest.
Odysseus – do you know of him?

ODYSSEUS

Er . . . I've heard his name, of course.

EUMEAUS

A true king. And with vast wealth –
land, cattle, crops, an army, a sailing fleet . . .

But he's missing, presumed dead.
Twenty years in his absence I've tended his flocks
while the household's gone to rack and ruin.

ODYSSEUS

Does he have family? A widow, perhaps.

EUMAEUS

Penelope – loyal as the moon to the earth.
But she can't hold out much longer.
Keeping those suitors at bay – it's like holding back a
   flood.

ODYSSEUS

No children to take up his role?

EUMAEUS

A fine son, Telemachus. He's abroad
in search of his father – or his father's grave.
There's a rumour he's back on the island,
but that's hope talking. Here, have a bowl of stew.

ODYSSEUS

You're a kind man. You offer me shelter and food
without even asking my name.

EUMAEUS

I can see who you are.

ODYSSEUS

You can?

EUMAEUS

You're a working man like me.
You've got a sun-beaten face and leather hands
and enough dirt under your finger nails to plant corn in.
You're old – older than me even!
You've lived a hard life under the stars – right?

ODYSSEUS

Right.

EUMAEUS

We're two of a kind then. What else is there to know?
How's the stew?

ODYSSEUS

Everything I need. Bless you.

Outside, the dogs are excited.

Sounds like another stranger coming to your door.

EUMAEUS

More like a friend, I'd say, listening to those dogs –
sounds like they're kissing his feet!
Another herdsmen from over the hill, I'd guess.

There is a knock at the door.

Come in. Always room for one more.

Telemachus opens the door and stands in the door frame.

(*delirious with excitement*)
Telemachus Telemachus Telemachus!

TELEMACHUS

Eumaeus – loyal and trusted friend.

EUMAEUS

Telemachus Telemachus Telemachus!
Give thanks to the Gods and planets.
Telemachus Telemachus Telemachus!
Give thanks to a thousand stars.
Ho! Telemachus – wasn't I just singing his praises?

ODYSSEUS

To the sky.

TELEMACHUS
Who's the old man?

EUMAEUS
A wanderer – hungry and out of breath.
Telemachus Telemachus Telemachus!
A miracle – I'd only a minute ago spoken your name!
Tell him, hadn't I just this second spoken his name?

ODYSSEUS
Not more than a moment since.

EUMAEUS
Tell me all about your trip. But first
this calls for a slap-up feast!
I'll skewer the juiciest pig in the pen.
Crank up the fire while I'm outside.

Oh, it's good to see you, young man.
Telemachus Telemachus Telemachus . . .
Ha!

He goes outside, chuckling to himself.

TELEMACHUS
Well, I haven't seen happiness like that for a long while.

ODYSSEUS
You've put him in high spirits. He adores you.

TELEMACHUS
It's inherited glory. He adores my father more.

ODYSSEUS
Your father?

TELEMACHUS
Odysseus.

ODYSSEUS
    Of course. Any news of him on your travels?

TELEMACHUS
    Rumours. Gossip. Nothing solid.
    I've told myself I might never see him again.
    I'm prepared for the worst.

ODYSSEUS
    Would you know him if he returned?

TELEMACHUS
    I was only a baby when he left.
    But they say he stands out. They say he's a man
    above and beyond ordinary men, and unmistakable.

ODYSSEUS
    You must . . . miss him.

TELEMACHUS
    It hurts. A physical pain.

ODYSSEUS
    He must miss you too, a fine son.

TELEMACHUS (*upset*)
    If his heart still beats in his chest.

ODYSSEUS
    I apologize. I'm only an old stranger. I've overstepped the
        mark.

TELEMACHUS
    Your words weren't meant to harm, though.
    You have a kindness that shines through.
    I'll . . . help Eumaeus catch his pig.

Telemachus leaves the hut.

ODYSSEUS (*to himself, his voice full of emotion*)
My son, my living flesh. My miraculous son.

Athena appears from nowhere.

ATHENA
Do you hear me, Odysseus?

ODYSSEUS
Voices in the air?
No, I can't make out . . . who is it, standing in the dark
corner?
Show your face.

ATHENA
Don't you recognize your lucky Goddess, your guiding
light?

ODYSSEUS
Athena – what if they see you?
You gave me this disguise – now you'll blow my cover.

ATHENA
It's time your son knows you for who you are.
Then the two of you can hatch a plan –
you'll know what to say, I've planted the seed in your
head.
Time's running down.

Here – I fling magic at you.
I throw you back the strength in your bones,
and the colour in your hair,
and the smoothness of your skin,
the straightness in your spine,
your supple limbs,

and here – here's fire for your eyes,
and a worthy shirt for your shoulders.

Who wouldn't recognize you now, handsome Odysseus?

ODYSSEUS

One minute I'm a dull old man,
the next I'm shining like a king.
What will my son say?

ATHENA

Make the most of your appearance – it's just a fleeting
  glimpse.
Here comes Telemachus. I'll dissolve into air again.

Telemachus returns to the hut.

TELEMACHUS

There's a comical sight.
Those grunters are like greased lightning, and . . .

What's happening here? Your skin, your face . . .

ODYSSEUS

Don't be afraid, Telemachus.

TELEMACHUS

This is freakish. Supernatural.

ODYSSEUS

I'm the same person.

TELEMACHUS

No, you were a mortal – an old, withered man.
Now – you glow. Like . . . like a God.

ODYSSEUS

I'm no God – just a man transformed by the touch of a
   Goddess.
Look at me, Telemachus.
Who am I?

TELEMACHUS

You're a trickster. You'll put a spell on me.

ODYSSEUS

It's no trick. Look at me.
Who am I?

TELEMACHUS

You deceive me.

ODYSSEUS

LOOK AT ME. Look at me, Telemachus, my son.

TELEMACHUS

. . . Your son?

ODYSSEUS

What did you say, that Odysseus is unmistakable?
Then don't mistake him. Recognize him at once.

TELEMACHUS (*stunned*)

That's what they say. What I've always been told.

ODYSSEUS

See me for who I am. You'll see no other Odysseus.

I hold out a father's hand to you, Telemachus.
Take it. Take it, Telemachus.

Let the bond be remade. Let this family begin again.

TELEMACHUS
　Father? Father?

Telemachus breaks down in tears in front of his father.

ODYSSEUS
　Weep with me, my son. Weep with me.

　Then swear an oath – to keep my return a secret.

TELEMACHUS
　Father. My father.

ODYSSEUS
　Swear an oath, Telemachus,
　there's a bloody feud to be won.

TELEMACHUS
　But the two of us can't settle it alone.
　Forty or fifty men sprawl in our home.
　I need to use your name to recruit an armed force.

ODYSSEUS
　Swear!
　An absolute oath – a bond between father and son.
　Go to the palace but tell no one – not even Penelope
　　herself.
　I'll appear as a beggar again –
　if I'm insulted and abused just bite your lip.
　Play along with the deceit.

TELEMACHUS
　Twenty years you've been out of our lives.
　Now I've got to pretend you don't exist.

ODYSSEUS
　Swear an oath, Telemachus – everything depends on it.

TELEMACHUS
    I swear.

ODYSSEUS
    Save whatever you're feeling – anger, bitterness,
        impatience . . .
    I'll give the signal when the time comes.
    Then pick up a spear and a sword and stand beside me,
    and let rip.

ATHENA
  Father?

ZEUS
  Yes, indeed. I was watching. Really very touching.

ATHENA
  You scoff at my intervention!

ZEUS (*genuinely moved*)
  Not at all – I mean every word of it.
  The love between a parent and child – it's . . . a rarity.
  Without condition. Uncompromised. A kind of purity.
  And mortals – they have their shortcomings, millions of
      them,
  but they show their feelings.
  And when they do . . .

  Come here, child, let me hold you.

ATHENA (*embarrassed*)
  Father.

ZEUS (*somewhat rejected*)
  Yes, you're right. Outward displays of affection. Frowned
      upon.

ATHENA
  No, I didn't mean to . . .

ZEUS (*becoming Godlike again*)
  Frowned upon, I said.
  In any case, your work there isn't finished.
  Unless it's just some hobby you've tired of?

ATHENA

I'll see it through right to the finish.
I'll stand at his shoulder to the very end.

ZEUS

To intervene when insult and indignity come his way?

ATHENA

Exactly right.

ZEUS

Exactly wrong.

ATHENA

But father . . .

ZEUS

Take advice from someone who knows about retribution
    and revenge.

Let his flesh soak up as much bitterness as it can take.
Let his nerves come close to overloading with pain.
Let him stare into the dark, let him brush with terror,
stand eyelash to eyelash with fear.

ATHENA

How much more can he stomach?

ZEUS

As much as it takes. Then he'll turn it to rage.
He'll need all the fury he can summon.
Anything short of total agony, utter hurt, and he'll fall
    short.

Let him suffer first, or he'll fail.
Let the sound of his wife's sadness eat into his heart.

PENELOPE'S BED-CHAMBER

PENELOPE
And bring them home safe.
Land them safe in Ithaca.
My husband and my son.
Gods of the heavens, I beg of you.

EURYCLEIA (*entering the room*)
Sorry, ma'am, I didn't mean to interrupt your prayers.

PENELOPE
No, I was talking to myself.

EURYCLEIA
I can come back.

PENELOPE
Stay and freshen the room with flowers. I need some air.

Penelope goes out onto the balcony. Below her, the suitors are plotting.

ANTINOUS
Any sign of the son yet?

EURYMACHUS
Neither hide nor hair. We've got prying eyes
all over the island, but they've seen nothing.

AMPHINOMUS
He's getting help from above – that's my theory.

ANTINOUS
He'll need it if any of my men catch him.

PENELOPE (*to herself*)
　　Bloodsuckers. Merciless, heartless creatures.

AMPHINOMUS
　　What if he turns up here?

ANTINOUS
　　What if he does?

AMPHINOMUS
　　We can't run him through with a spear on his own doorstep.

ANTINOUS
　　You're a flaky one.

AMPHINOMUS
　　I want this matter resolved as much as anyone,
　　But to cut him down in front of his mother . . .

EURYMACHUS
　　I'll quite happily tear him organ from organ.

PENELOPE (*unable to contain her anger*)
　　You VIOLATE me.

The suitors are shocked into silence.

　　You, Amphinomus – I thought better of you.

AMPHINOMUS
　　My lady, I . . .

PENELOPE
　　Eurymachus – your parents raised a brute.
　　And you, Antinous – you're inhuman
　　and sadistic – right down to your roots.
　　They say you're the finest young man
　　on the island – what must the worst be like?

Your father came here once, on the run.
He'd fallen in with a bad lot. Angry mobs
wanted him strung up from a post,
but Odysseus took him in, harboured him,
helped him ride out the storm.
Now you trash the house of Odysseus,
and drool over his grieving wife,
and make plans to butcher his son.
(*tearful*)
You're monsters. You're breaking my heart.
Do you understand? Get out of this house.
Get out. GET OUT. GET OUT.

Penelope rushes back into her room, slams the door and
collapses on the bed in tears.

EURYCLEIA
My lady! My lady!

PENELOPE
Leave me.

EURYCLEIA
But my lady . . .

PENELOPE
Leave me – do you hear?

EURYCLEIA
As you wish, my lady.
Except, if you'd only turn you head this way,
let your eyes do some seeing instead of all these
    waterworks.

PENELOPE
How dare you. Leave me alone with my tears.

TELEMACHUS (*gently*)
Mother.

Penelope bites back her tears to listen again for the voice.

Mother.

PENELOPE
Telemachus.

EURYCLEIA (*giddy*)
I bumped into him walking up the back steps.
Up the back steps!
I kissed his face and his hands like he was my own!
Look at him – I threw myself into his arms!

PENELOPE
Leave us, Eurycleia.

EURYCLEIA
Well, I only . . . In the circumstances . . . Yes, my lady.

Threw myself into his arms I did . . .
Up the back stairs indeed . . .

She leaves the room.

PENELOPE
You sneak home as secretly as you left.

TELEMACHUS
Is that the welcome I get?

PENELOPE
You stole away with no word of where you were going or
  why.
Against my will.
You left me here on my own.

TELEMACHUS

Inaction was killing me.
I had to go in search of news of my father –
your husband, Odysseus.

PENELOPE

So spit it out. Is he dead?

TELEMACHUS (*mumbling*)

No hard news.
A story that said he was trapped by the nymph
Calypso . . .

PENELOPE

Held in another woman's arms?

TELEMACHUS

Held there by force.
And rumours of battles and skirmishes on the way home
from Troy . . .

PENELOPE

Don't think I'm a stone.
Don't think my heart didn't fly up when I heard your
voice.
They were plotting to kill you –
I thought you'd walked straight onto their spears.

TELEMACHUS

I'm no longer a child, mother.

PENELOPE

Then give me news of your father.

TELEMACHUS

I have nothing to tell. I . . . can't say.

PENELOPE
So leave me to grieve. Nothing has changed.
I'll wind myself in this shroud of bedsheets again.

TELEMACHUS
Don't languish.
Wash with water instead of tears.
Put on clean robes, go to the roof and pray to Zeus.

I have business to attend to.
Be glad that I'm alive.

Laughter and cheering comes from the hall below.
Telemachus leaves the room and addresses the suitors from
the balcony.

Up here. No, not a ghost.
Not dead – sorry to disappoint you.
Still got your heads in the trough, I see?
Well, eat up, eat up.
We're famed for our hospitality,
we won't turn anyone away.
We won't give you the satisfaction.

Cooks – more meat on the spit.
Carver – double each portion – good thick slices.
Waiters – be quicker with the plates.
You with the jar of wine – don't stint,
charge every glass to the brink.
Slake them to the last drop.
Feed them to the last grain.

Penelope can hear Telemachus' words from her chamber.

PENELOPE (*to herself*)
Odysseus – come home. Come home for your wife and
    son.

[224]

ARGOS

Athena has restored Odysseus' disguise. Still believing him to be a shipwrecked sailor from Crete, Eumaeus is escorting him towards the royal palace.

EUMAEUS

    All right there, old timer?

ODYSSEUS

    I'm just about managing, thanks.

EUMAEUS

    Not going too fast, am I? I'm no spring chicken myself
    but you've got a good number of years over me.

ODYSSEUS

    There's a few miles left in these old legs yet.

EUMAEUS

    What about Telemachus, eh?
    See – he doesn't know you from a hole in the road,
    but he only invites you down to his palace for a square
       meal –
    and you a perfect stranger, and hardly royalty – no
       offence and all that.
    He's a fine boy grown into a fine man.

ODYSSEUS

    His father would be proud of him.

EUMAEUS

    His heart would burst – believe me.
    That's one reunion I hope to live to see.

Melanthius, another herder, crosses their path.

MELANTHIUS
Well, look who it isn't.

EUMAEUS (*to Odysseus*)
Ignore him. He's no better than me.

MELANTHIUS
Eumaeus, loyal swineherd to Odysseus.
So who's the clapped-out old creature you're taking to
market today?

EUMAEUS
I'll not trade insults with you, Melanthius. Good day.

MELANTHIUS
I thought you were the creakiest pile of bones on the
whole island,
but this one takes the biscuit.
What a filth-bag.

EUMAEUS
Good day, Melanthius.

MELANTHIUS
Hey, beggar-man thing – are you dead or alive?

EUMAEUS
We're minding our own business, why don't you mind
yours?

MELANTHIUS
It is my business.
There's too many spongers and cadgers hanging around
without you towing one more into town.
If he comes to my house begging for scraps and crusts

[226]

he'll get a boot in the face,
then I'll slam his pilfering fingers in the door.
(*He hits Odysseus with his stick.*)
There's something for your troubles, you scum.
Get back to your shanty.

EUMAEUS

Leave him alone!

MELANTHIUS

Oh, do you want some too?

EUMAEUS

We're heading for the palace, if you must know.

MELANTHIUS

The palace! Those suitors will rip him to pieces just for
    sport.
They'll break stools over his head,
they'll use his teeth for dice.

EUMAEUS (*to Odysseus*)

Take no heed. Just let it go.

MELANTHIUS (*his voice disappearing behind them*)
The palace – oh that's a good one.
They'll use his backside for target practice.
They'll push a hook up his arse and pull him inside
    out . . .

EUMAEUS

No respect. No consideration. It never used to be like this.

A dog barks and whines pitifully.

Well, would you look at that sad sight,
a sign of the times if ever there was one.

ODYSSEUS

What's a noble breed of dog like that doing sleeping on a pile of dung?

EUMAEUS

You might well ask. That's Argos. Odysseus' dog.

ODYSSEUS

Argos?

EUMAEUS

Trained him as a pup, he did. Taught him to hunt.
But then he sailed for Troy – never saw him quarter a field or bring down a hare going at full lick.
I swear he was the best hound ever. Now look at him.

ODYSSEUS

Come here, boy.

EUMAEUS

Jumping with fleas and ticks.

ODYSSEUS

There's a boy. There's a boy.

EUMAEUS

Eyes all gummed up, ears weeping from bites and cuts.

ODYSSEUS

You're a beautiful feller. There's a boy.

EUMAEUS

Gone in the legs. Horrible to watch. Well, he likes you right enough.

ODYSSEUS

There now, rest your head, old boy. There now. There now.

EUMAEUS

He's a tired one. Poor thing can hardly stand.
Likes the taste of your hand though. Must be the salt.

ODYSSEUS

Lie down, lie down. There's a boy. Lie down.
You sleep. It's over now. Lie down. You sleep. There's a
boy.

The dog stops breathing.

EUMAEUS

Is he gone?

ODYSSEUS

He's at rest now.

EUMAEUS

It's a blessing.
Only had eyes for his master.

You've got a gentle way with animals, old timer, I'll say
that.

ODYSSEUS (*whispering*)

Sleep now, Argos. Loyal friend.

Music and laughter drifts towards them from the palace.

Someone's having a good time.

EUMAEUS

The Palace of Odysseus. Magnificent, eh?

ODYSSEUS

Like a mirage.

EUMAEUS

Not as splendid as it was

before those mongrels made themselves at home, but still
a fine spectacle.
Imagine coming home – seeing that after twenty years at
war and at sea.
Imagine a feeling like that.

ODYSSEUS
Yes, imagine.

EUMAEUS
Well, come on, the main door's standing open. Don't
dawdle.

ODYSSEUS ENTERS HIS PALACE

EUMAEUS

Take a seat, old feller. Look, there's noble Telemachus,
still doing his duty, hosting this pack of free-loaders.

ODYSSEUS

Shall I approach him myself?

EUMAEUS

Why not – he invited you here. He won't have forgotten.

Odysseus approaches Telemachus.

TELEMACHUS (*hushed*)

Father.

ODYSSEUS (*whispering*)

Don't let them see through our pretence. Act accordingly.
I need to test these suitors man by man – but how?

TELEMACHUS

Here – take this bowl around. Beg from them one by one.
You'll get the measure of them by their response.

Odysseus takes a bowl and approaches the suitors in turn.

ODYSSEUS (*to Amphinomus*)

Any crusts to spare, young man, sir? Anything going
begging?

AMPHINOMUS

Who's this, then?

ODYSSEUS

Just an old man with a grumbling belly.

AMPHINOMUS

Here, take these ribs – you can dig the marrow from
them. Now shoo.

ODYSSEUS

Very kind, my young sir. God bless you.

He approaches Eurymachus.

Sir, if you'll beg my pardon.
Can you spare a scrap or two from your plate?

EURYMACHUS

What – fuck off – I'm eating. Whatever happened to good
manners?

ODYSSEUS

I'm ashamed to be asking. Don't make it worse for me,
sir.
Just a crust or a half-chewed bone or a burnt sausage.
My belly thinks my throat's been cut.

EURYMACHUS

It might come true.
You're a scavenger, whoever you are, and a filthy one at
that.
Well, it's worth a lump of gristle just to keep you away.
There – on the floor – where the dogs eat. Now vanish.

Odysseus approaches Antinous.

ODYSSEUS

Fine young sir, if I could trouble you . . .

ANTINOUS

Look what the wind blew in.

ODYSSEUS

If you could spare a morsel of meat for a man in his later
years.

ANTINOUS

Did someone leave the gates of the graveyard open?

The suitors laugh.

ODYSSEUS

I apologize if my appearance offends you.

ANTINOUS

Appearance? It's your existence I object to.
Now stop breathing on me and crawl back in your hole.

AMPHINOMUS

Don't be ruthless, Antinous. It's only human to be hungry.

ANTINOUS

This swamp donkey isn't human. Who let him in?

EUMAEUS

He came with me.

EURYMACHUS

And who are you?

EUMAEUS

Eumaeus, loyal herdsman to Odysseus.

ANTINOUS

A pig-man – that figures! One swine leading another.

ODYSSEUS

Just a bite, sir. That kidney on your plate – you wouldn't
miss it.

ANTINOUS (*flaring with anger*)
You ignorant, shameless scrounger.
Get your loathsome hand away from my meal.
Pig-man, don't you think there are enough mouths to feed
without bringing beggars into the hall?

EUMAEUS
Aye, and you're one of them yourself. What's the
difference?
You and your lot – you're a swarm of locusts.

ANTINOUS
You impertinent wretch.

TELEMACHUS
Ignore him, Eumaeus. Don't waste your breath.

EUMAEUS
He's got some neck, though. Him and his friends
leaching the blood from this proud house,
then he turns round and tells another man not to beg.
Outrageous!

ODYSSEUS
Even the shell from your egg, sir.
The cow's horn, the billy goat's beard – anything.

ANTINOUS
You're right. You're so right. Where are my manners?
Here, take a seat. This stool I'm sitting on – you can have
it.
(*He smashes the stool over Odysseus' head.*)
Right across your skull.

AMPHINOMUS
Antinous, for God's sake calm down.

EURYMACHUS

Keep out of it. Let him have his say.

AMPHINOMUS

It's an offence in the eyes of the Gods to mistreat a
stranger.

EURYMACHUS

The Gods don't care about him.
If they did, he wouldn't be a good-for-nothing beggar.

TELEMACHUS (*under his breath, attending to Odysseus*)

Father, are you hurt?

ODYSSEUS

Ignore it.

TELEMACHUS

I won't stand for this any longer. I'll kill Antinous right
now.

ODYSSEUS

If you want what's best for us you'll swallow your pride.
Now get away from me.
(*hisses*)
Get away.

ANTINOUS

Fetch me another seat, somebody.
And throw that flea-ridden dosser into the street.

PENELOPE (*from the balcony*)

As long as this is the house of Odysseus I'll say how
guests are treated.

ODYSSEUS (*hushed, captivated by the first sight of his wife*)

Penelope.

TELEMACHUS (*hushed, to Odysseus*)
Now it's your turn to hold your tongue.

PENELOPE
Give that stranger a bandage for his head.
We treat visitors here with courtesy – you should know,
you've tested our hospitality to the edge of bankruptcy.

And you've strained my nerves and my heart to breaking
point.
Beyond breaking point.

ANTINOUS
All we want is resolution to this situation . . .

PENELOPE (*cutting through him*)
I've reached a decision.
The morning Odysseus sailed for Troy
he held me by the wrist. Wait for me, he said.
Wait until our baby son is a man with a beard on his chin.
Then for the sake of yourself, for the sake of everything,
choose another man.

That day has come.

TELEMACHUS (*under his breath*)
No, mother.

ODYSSEUS (*hushed*)
Let her speak.

PENELOPE
It's time to . . . give up the ghost.
I'm worn down.
Why you should want me – empty and bitter and cold,
all my womanly beauty drained by grief – Zeus only knows.
But I'll honour my husband's will. I'll marry one of you.

There is agreement, relief and self-congratulation among the suitors.

AMPHINOMUS
My lady, gracious queen . . .

PENELOPE
Time was when a suitor would court his lady with
    presents.
Lay wondrous offerings at her feet.
Outbid his rivals with promises of wealth.
Shower the family of the bride-to-be with shimmering
    gifts.

TELEMACHUS (*aside*)
She lines her pockets into the bargain.

ODYSSEUS (*hushed response*)
No, she fleeces them. Let them pay.

ANTINOUS
My lady, your change of heart is most welcome and most
    timely.
And now that common sense has taken hold,
we'll court you the way that tradition demands.
We'll bring gifts. Pile them to the ceiling if need be.

And may the best man win!

The suitors cheer.

PENELOPE
But leave me in peace now.
Go home to your houses – let me have one last night
to prepare, and make my peace, and accept my loss.

AMPHINOMUS
We'll grant you that, of course.

[237]

The suitors begin to pack up their bags and leave the house.

PENELOPE

Eumaeus?

EUMAEUS

You call for me, my lady?

PENELOPE

Come here and answer me a question.

Eumaeus makes his way to Penelope.

The old man who begged from the table, who is he?

EUMAEUS

A stranger, shipwrecked coming from Crete,
washed up on Ithaca's shore.
He knocked on my door and I took him in.

PENELOPE

From Crete?
The trade winds might have whispered my husband's
    name in his ears.
Tell him to expect my company.
I'll speak to him in due course.

*

Later. The house of Odysseus stands quiet.

EUMAEUS

Old man, here she comes. Dust yourself down.

PENELOPE

Don't stand up – please.
Those suitors brought shame on this house
with their rudeness towards you. You deserve to sit.

[238]

ODYSSEUS

All I've heard of your kindness is true. And your beauty.

PENELOPE

Where are you from, stranger?

ODYSSEUS

Lady, don't ask me the name of my country.
Don't ask me to crack open my heart in front of you.
You've troubles enough in this house without my sob-
story.
I'll weep, and you'll think me drunk and maudlin.

PENELOPE

Nothing could take my spirits any lower.

ODYSSEUS

You've suffered and suffered – your face tells me as much.

PENELOPE

When Odysseus, my husband, sailed for Troy,
he took my soul with him.

Then the vultures started to circle.
I held those suitors off for long enough,
weaving a shroud for my husband's father,
telling them I wouldn't wed until the long fine threads
were interlaced and woven tight.

Then unpicked it every night! For three years it was my
alibi.

ODYSSEUS

A brilliant scheme.

PENELOPE

But they found me out. The maidservants were two-faced.
Now there's no more web to weave. No escape.

ODYSSEUS

Lady, you've been honest with me, now I'll say something about myself.

My homeland is Crete.

PENELOPE

I know of it.

ODYSSEUS

It was there I met him. Odysseus.

PENELOPE

You met my husband? How long ago?

ODYSSEUS

Years and years, I'm afraid.

He was making for Troy when the wind blew him off course.

He moored in the harbour to escape the storm.

One evening he ate in my house.

Then after two weeks, with the wind back to right again, he sailed.

That was the last I saw of him.

PENELOPE

He ate in your house?

ODYSSEUS

Sat as close to me as you are sitting right now.

PENELOPE

If it's true, tell me what clothes he wore?

ODYSSEUS

Lady, it's difficult. Twenty years – the memory fades.

PENELOPE

No one forgets Odysseus. What did he wear?

ODYSSEUS

Well, let me conjure up the picture of him standing at my
door.

A blue cloak. No, purple. A purple cloak.

PENELOPE

Go on.

ODYSSEUS

With a double fold – that's right.

A purple cloak with a double fold.

Pinned with a brooch, and on the brooch

the image of a deer or faun,

being dragged to the ground by a dog, a hunting hound.

I admired it. Well, all did.

If I close my eyes I see it clear as daylight now.

PENELOPE (*moved by the account of her husband*)

I gave him that cloak.

I folded it, fastened that pin.

It was the last time I touched him.

ODYSSEUS

I'm sorry to have opened the wound again.

PENELOPE

It never closed.

You gave my husband shelter a long way from home.

It's the least I can do to give you the same. Eurycleia?

EURYCLEIA

Yes, my lady. Coming, my lady.

PENELOPE

Here's our old nurse. She suckled Odysseus himself.

EURYCLEIA

That I did, my lady. He fed at my breast.

PENELOPE

Make up a couch for our guest.

EURYCLEIA

I will.

PENELOPE

And wash him. Bathe his feet.

ODYSSEUS

I'm fine here on the hearth rug – I'm used to roughing it.

PENELOPE

I won't hear of you not being comfortable under my roof.
And let her bathe your feet – you'll feel better for it.
I'll be in the upper room. I have prayers to say.

Eurycleia kneels at Odysseus' feet with a bowl of water.

EURYCLEIA

Come on, off with those sandals.
My, these feet have squashed some miles under them.
Not damaged though. Not a nail broken. Good strong
    ankles.

You're very alike, you know, you and Odysseus.

ODYSSEUS

People have commented on the resemblance.

EURYCLEIA

Alike in height and width. Similar voices.
I thought you were far older, 'scuse me saying,
but these are a younger man's feet. Same size as his, I'd say.

ODYSSEUS

Have you finished?

EURYCLEIA

I've only just started – relax. Lie back.
He liked his feet bathed, you know.

ODYSSEUS

Did he?

EURYCLEIA

Like washing his troubles away, he'd say.
He had a scar on his leg.

ODYSSEUS

Really?

EURYCLEIA

I'll say he did. Went hunting when he was a lad,
and a wild boar comes tearing out of a thicket.
He killed it with a spear, bang! –
but not before it gouged the flesh with its tusk.

ODYSSEUS

Thank you, you can stop now.

EURYCLEIA

A real gash, it was. Just below the knee.
No, on the other leg, just about there, just . . .

She drops his leg. The bronze bowl of water turns over onto the floor.

EURYCLEIA

All the Gods and all the stars in heaven – it's you.

ODYSSEUS

Be quiet, Eurycleia.

EURYCLEIA
    It's my lord and master.
    Dear child – it's you, Odysseus. It's Odysseus.

ODYSSEUS (*almost violently*)
    Keep it closed, old nurse.
    You suckled me into life – don't get me killed now.
    This stays a secret until those suitors are dead,
    or, as I live and breathe, I'll have to finish you as well,
    along with those other servants and maids who've double-
        crossed us.

PENELOPE (*from afar*)
    What's going on?

EURYCLEIA
    I'll be as silent as a lump of iron.
    I'll be as silent as a stone, trapped in a block of ice, buried
        under snow.

ODYSSEUS
    See to it.

EURYCLEIA (*hushed, but excited*)
    And when your hands have finished with those suitors,
    bang! bang! bang!
    I'll point out the turncoats in this house.
    I'll point them out with my own hand . . .

PENELOPE (*entering*)
    Nurse – did you spill the water?
    Your old hands are growing weak . . .

ODYSSEUS
    No, it was my fault. She soothed me to sleep,
    then I kicked out in a dream.

EURYCLEIA

I'll run and fetch a cloth to mop up the mess.
And blankets for a bed. Excuse me, ma'am. Sir.

Eurycleia exits.

PENELOPE

I have a dream – the same dream every night.
Are you someone who knows the meaning of dreams?

ODYSSEUS

Dreams are hard to fathom. What happens in yours?

PENELOPE

I have twenty white geese in the house – pets, really.
In the dream, an eagle swoops from the sky
and breaks the neck of every one with its hooked beak.
What does it mean?

ODYSSEUS

It's a good sign, isn't it?
Golden Odysseus will swoop on the house
and slay the suitors – isn't that what the dream says?

PENELOPE

I clung to that thought for a long time –
woke every morning full of hope. But I see now I was
    wrong.
Now it's a nightmare – I sleep in cold sweat.

Well, tomorrow waits in the east – an evil day.
I have an archery contest in mind – what do you think?

ODYSSEUS

With the winner taking your hand?

PENELOPE
To sort the wheat from the chaff. The men from the boys.

ODYSSEUS
It sounds perfect to me. Appropriate.
Whoever claims you as his prize must be no ordinary
man.

PENELOPE
Goodnight, stranger from Crete.

Penelope leaves.

ODYSSEUS
My lady. My Penelope.

Eurycleia returns.

EURYCLEIA
Here's enough blankets to keep a horse warm.
Need anything else, *stranger*?

ODYSSEUS
Nothing.

EURYCLEIA
Then I'll say goodnight. *Stranger!*

ODYSSEUS
Don't squeal, Eurycleia. Keep the secret.

EURYCLEIA
My lips are stitched together. Mmnnnn!

Odysseus beds down for the night.

ODYSSEUS (*to himself*)
Be strong, Odysseus. Be iron-hearted.
Don't let doubts gnaw away at your courage all night.

ATHENA

Awake, or talking in your sleep, Odysseus?

ODYSSEUS

Athena – silver-eyed Goddess.
I thought . . . I thought you'd deserted me when I most
needed you.

ATHENA

Desertion?
The Gods don't waver – hesitation and doubt are human
failings.

ODYSSEUS

Doubt and hesitation are in me tonight.
There must be fifty suitors at least.
Do you promise to fight at my shoulder?
Does almighty Zeus lend his support to this venture?

ATHENA

Go to the heavy door of your wife's chamber, Odysseus.
Don't enter – just listen.

ODYSSEUS

Skulk in the corridors of my house, eavesdropping –
what kind of plan is that? That's no promise.
Athena? Athena?

*Odysseus climbs the steps and stands outside Penelope's
chamber. He puts his ear to the door.*

I hear nothing. The sound of sleeping.

Penelope begins to murmur.

My wife. Praying. Saying her prayers. A sweet sound.

PENELOPE (*from inside the room*)
Artemis, hear me.
Aphrodite, hear me.
Hera and Athena, all women of Olympus,
hear this woman's request.

Take away my life.

ODYSSEUS (*to himself*)
No, Penelope.

PENELOPE
Let an arrow fly at my life.
Let me join my husband in death.
Sleep was once my escape,
now dreams worm into my mind.

Let oblivion draw its dark sheet over me.
Goddesses of Olympus,
lay a weight on my heart now, and let me sleep.

ODYSSEUS (*to himself*)
Athena – you'd have me suffer more,
listen to my wife pleading for death.

Well, now doubts and hesitation are blown away.
Tomorrow I'll rage. Tomorrow I'll flare and blaze.
Beware those who stand in the blast.
I come alive – every atom of me ignites now with fury.

THE STRINGING OF THE BOW

The next morning. Loud, boastful and already drinking, the suitors are gathered in the hall for the day of reckoning. Also present in the hall are Telemachus, Eurycleia, Eumaeus and Odysseus, still in disguise.

ODYSSEUS (*under his breath, to Telemachus*)
Did you empty the weapons from the locker and hide them?

TELEMACHUS
All hidden out of harm's way.

ODYSSEUS
Remember, do nothing until I give the signal.
The timing is everything.

EURYMACHUS
Telemachus, no hard feelings, eh?
You're not losing a mother. You're gaining a step-father.

The suitors laugh.

TELEMACHUS
A thought that hadn't escaped me, Eurymachus.

ANTINOUS
Don't look so worried. We won't be too hard on you.
But if I'm the chosen one, you'll have to be sent abroad.
Some island with only wolves and bears for company.
Toughen you up.

EURYMACHUS
It's what his father would have wanted.

ANTINOUS
Exactly. And we must do right by the father
if we're to step into his boots, slip between his sheets!
So don't think we'll neglect you, Telemachus.
On the contrary. What say you, Amphinomus?

AMPHINOMUS
I won't goad the son of the woman I want to marry.
But I've got to admit to feeling excited – even giddy.
Let it happen! I've got a lucky feeling about this day.

EUMAEUS (*making an announcement*)
The queen will address you.

They carry on talking.

TELEMACHUS
THE QUEEN WILL ADDRESS YOU. If you're quite
ready.

They fall silent as Penelope enters the room.

PENELOPE
Your gifts are stacked high in the lobby.
They are duly noted.

But I won't be bought by material goods alone.

EURYMACHUS
What's this – more time wasting?

EUMAEUS
Let her finish.

PENELOPE
A contest. Eumaeus, raise the weapon for all to see.
This was my husband's bow – a gift from Iphitos.
He didn't carry it into war but left it here in his house.

Surely you didn't think I'd marry for money alone –
throw myself at the man with the deepest pockets
or the widest fields or the greatest flocks to his name.
The man who takes my husband's place must be strong –
strong enough to lace this heavy bow.
And steady enough to lift it, take aim,
let an arrow pass between those twelve axe-shafts – look –
planted in line for the occasion.
And brave – steely enough to contemplate failure.

So who here has the courage?

EURYMACHUS
    This wasn't the plan. This wasn't what we expected.

TELEMACHUS
    Spontaneity was never your strong point, was it?

EURYMACHUS
    You little runt . . .

TELEMACHUS
    Or you, Antinous? Nothing to say for a change?
    Maybe you haven't got what it takes?
    Maybe you don't have the nerve? The guts? The balls?

ANTINOUS (*keeping cool*)
    This . . . is an unexpected turn of events.

EUMAEUS
    Look at them, blown over by a little change in the breeze.
    They're not fit to marry one of my pigs.

ANTINOUS
    You keep your mouth closed, swineherd.

TELEMACHUS
    None of you? No?
    Then I'll lace it myself. Why not? Eumaeus, pass the bow.

Eumaeus grunts under the weight.

ANTINOUS
    It proves nothing.

TELEMACHUS
    Spoken like a true coward.

EURYMACHUS
    So what will you do if you win – marry your own
        mother?

TELEMACHUS
    Lead her away from you rabble.

He grapples with the bow.

    Look, it already bends.

EURYMACHUS
    You'll give yourself an accident, Telemachus.

TELEMACHUS (*trying to flex the bow*)
    It gives to my strength. It gives and gives.

EUMAEUS
    They say a bow like this only yields to its true owner.

TELEMACHUS
    An inch more. Just an inch more . . .

ODYSSEUS (*under his breath*)
    No, Telemachus. Don't.

The bow finally springs apart in his hands.

EUMAEUS
Hard luck, Telemachus. At least you made the effort.
Your father would have been proud, just as I am.

AMPHINOMUS (*carried away with excitement*)
Move aside.

ANTINOUS
You, Amphinomus. What's this sudden rush of blood to
the head?

AMPHINOMUS
Let me have the next attempt.
I see how it's done.
I'll string the bow and fire through the axes –

I can feel it – this is my moment.
(*He struggles with the bow.*)
Come on, give to me, give to me . . . Damn you!
(*amazed at his inability*)
I . . . couldn't. I really thought . . . Now I'm ashamed of
my failure.

EURYMACHUS
It wasn't in the stars. You've never been lucky,
Amphinomus –
I told you that when we played dice.

AMPHINOMUS (*broken*)
Not my destiny. I wonder what is, then?
I thought the path of my life led to this day.

EURYMACHUS
Give it to me. GIVE IT ME.
I feel a tide of energy.

(*He shouts at the bow.*)
COME ON. BEND, YOU STUBBORN
    CONTRAPTION . . .
(*He fights with the bow, trying to lace the string.*)
BEND FOR ME. I'LL BREAK YOUR SPINE.
I'LL BREAK YOU, YOU . . . NNNGGGNNRRRR.

The bow springs apart again. He throws it aside in disgust.

ODYSSEUS (*plainly*)
Let me try.

ANTINOUS
What – is this flea-bag still in the house?
I thought I'd had you thrown in the gutter.

TELEMACHUS
It isn't your house. You don't give the orders.

EUMAEUS
Shall I give him the bow?

ANTINOUS
Of course not. He's just a drifter, a no-mark.
This is the contest for the Queen of Ithaca –
not some shooting gallery at a travelling circus. Kick him
    outside.

PENELOPE
Give him the bow.

ANTINOUS
This is farcical.

PENELOPE
Give him the bow – what is there to lose?
If he succeeds I'm hardly going to marry him,

but I will kit him out with clothes and a sword for his
    journey.
And the rest of you suitors will be judged by his
    standards.
Give him the bow.

TELEMACHUS
    I sanction it.

PENELOPE
    Quite rightly.

TELEMACHUS
    And now, mother, go to your room.

PENELOPE
    What?
    I will not leave this hall until the outcome of this contest
        is . . .

TELEMACHUS
    You will take instruction from the man of the house!
    I have authority over the bow. I decide.
    Not another word. Go to your room.

*There is a piercing silence, before Penelope turns and walks
away. The door of her bed-chamber is slammed shut.*

    (*to Eumaeus*)
    Hand him the bow.

ODYSSEUS (*hushed, to Eumaeus*)
    Eumaeus, do you believe in Odysseus? Are you loyal to
        his name?

EUMAEUS
    To my dying day. To my dying breath.

ODYSSEUS
Then believe in me. Look in my face. Look at Odysseus.

EUMAEUS (*astonished*)
Master? My master? It can't be.

ODYSSEUS
You'll have the proof soon enough.
Go with Eurycleia. Lock all the doors. Keep my wife in her room.

ANTINOUS
Well, men, this should be worth watching.
More likely the bow will bend him!

ODYSSEUS
Oh yes, Antinous, you'll find this entertaining all right.

Look, the bow resists. It resists and resists.
Then suddenly . . . it gives.

The suitors are transfixed.

So I lace the length of gut.
(*plucking the bow*)
Listen, taut, like an instrument.
Do you hear that note – the sweet spot?
The sound of power waiting to be unleashed.
So much for strength.
Now steadiness – an arrow from the quiver, and I take aim.
The trick here is not to flinch, not to blink, not even to breathe,
then . . .

The arrow passes cleanly between the axes.

AMPHINOMUS

He did it. He did it!
A clean shot – not one of the axes clipped.

EURYMACHUS

Unbelievable.

ODYSSEUS

Telemachus, won't you join me on this platform?

TELEMACHUS

Congratulations, stranger. You have the strength of a bull,
and the steadiness of a rock, and a sniper's eye.

ODYSSEUS

And no fluke either. Look, I'll prove it again.

ANTINOUS

Don't point that thing at me, beggar man.

ODYSSEUS

Oh yes, Antinous. As you lift that glass to your lips
and swallow down a gulp of wine, a moving target
rises and falls in your throat. Your Adam's apple,
    Antinous.
Let the Gods guide this arrow straight to its mark.

*He shoots Antinous in the throat. There is uproar in the
hall. Some men shout that the doors are locked, others
that the weapon cupboards are empty.*

ODYSSEUS

You rabid mongrels. You vermin.
You thought Odysseus would never return.
You fouled my house. Polluted my family. Scandalized my
    name.

EURYMACHUS

    Odysseus, if it's really you, spare us. It was Antinous all
      along,
    his idea, his planning and scheming that kept us here.
    Spare us, Odysseus, you've killed the worst of us.
    That can be our lesson.

ODYSSEUS

    No, Eurymachus, your lesson is more painful to learn.

EURYMACHUS

    We'll give back everything we've taken. Bronze, gold,
    you name it. Just say the price and we'll pay, I promise.

ODYSSEUS

    All the money in the world wouldn't cover it.
    This is the only way your debt can be settled.

He fires an arrow into Eurymachus' chest.

AMPHINOMUS

    Not me, Odysseus. You heard how I spoke out.
    I was never happy with this situation, never comfortable.

TELEMACHUS (*driving a spear into his back*)
    But never as uncomfortable as now I'll bet,
    wearing a spear between your shoulder blades.

The chaos in the hall escalates.

ODYSSEUS (*loosing off arrows left, right and centre*)
    You'll all die. You'll die, and you'll die, and you'll die.
    It's nothing less than you deserve.
    It's better than you deserve!
    (*shouting*)
    And when Death asks who sent you to his gate,
    don't forget my name.
    Tell him ODYSSEUS, ODYSSEUS, ODYSSEUS!

REUNION

Eurycleia goes to Penelope's room. She is sleeping.

EURYCLEIA
My lady.

PENELOPE (*stirring*)
Is it over?

EURYCLEIA
Over, my lady.

PENELOPE
Over, then. So who shall I marry?

EURYCLEIA
Ah, there'll be no marriage for them that's already wed.

PENELOPE
Don't set me a riddle. Just tell me.

EURYCLEIA
Your husband is here, my lady.

PENELOPE
You antagonize me, Eurycleia.
It's only your age that saves you. Go away.

EURYCLEIA
No, my lady. You insult me. But you're forgiven.

PENELOPE
What did you say?

EURYCLEIA
It's a blood-bath down there, but one to savour.

The suitors are dead, slain by Odysseus.
He was the beggar-stranger!
I guessed it but no one else did, not even his wife.
(*suddenly*)
YOU'RE SAVED! GO TO HIM. GO TO HIM.

PENELOPE

You're twisting the knife, Eurycleia. Your mind's gone.
I won't have you in the house if . . .

Odysseus stands in the door. Athena has removed his disguise.

ODYSSEUS

Leave us, Eurycleia.

EURYCLEIA

Yes, master. Excuse me, my lady.
Ha!

Eurycleia leaves the room and a long silence follows.

PENELOPE

It's the height of rudeness to enter a lady's chamber.

ODYSSEUS

You recognize me now that I'm washed and robed.
You know who I am.

PENELOPE

Stranger, I could have you strung up for this impertinence.

ODYSSEUS

You know I'm real, Penelope.

Silence.

It's you who acts the stranger now.

The Gods on Olympus gave you a stubborn heart.
Twenty years I've been away, ten of them fighting a war,
ten more fighting my way back to this chamber, this door.
No other woman would hold back like you.

PENELOPE

Who are you? I don't know who you are.

ODYSSEUS

You know.

PENELOPE

I know very well what my husband looked like when he
    set sail.
But what does he look like now?
You're a stranger. You're unfamiliar. Unknown.

ODYSSEUS

Very well!
I won't set foot inside this sacred room.
I'll sleep outside on the floor. Tell the maid to make up a
    bed.

PENELOPE

Wait a moment. Wait, let me think.
You should be honoured for what you have done for us.
You should . . . sleep in his bed.

ODYSSEUS

Oh, recognition at last!

PENELOPE

But not in my room. Drag the bed outside –
this bed that Odysseus built.

ODYSSEUS (*in anger and confusion*)
What? What do you want me to do?
That bed won't budge an inch. It's not furniture,
it's carved from the bole of an olive tree.
Its branches were stripped, it was planed flat,
stones were set in its wood, doors were added
and posts and a canopy over the top, its grain
was inlaid with silver and gold thread.

It wasn't carried here from a carpenter's shed,
that bed still has roots in the ground.

This room was built around that bed.

That marriage bed is the corner-stone of the whole house.

Penelope begins to weep

I shouldn't have raised my voice.

PENELOPE
Odysseus.

ODYSSEUS
I shouldn't have . . . I'll keep away . . .

PENELOPE
Only my husband knows the truth about this bed.
Only my husband. Oh Odysseus, my Odysseus.

They embrace and weep.

Come to me, Odysseus. Don't hate my stubbornness.
How should a woman know a man after twenty years?
How should a wife know her husband after that long?
Impostors have come here, men pretending to be you.
But no one has come close, Odysseus, do you hear?
It's only my stubborn heart that has kept us alive.

Only two people know the secret of this bed.

ODYSSEUS

This bed that I built – it proves who I am.

PENELOPE

And proves my faithfulness.

ODYSSEUS

And proves my trust.
And proves my heart, which ached all these endless years.

PENELOPE

You're home now, my Odysseus.

ODYSSEUS

You are my home, Penelope. You are my Ithaca.

OLYMPUS

ZEUS

> You fought like a warrior, Athena. Like you were born
> to it.

ATHENA

> It gave me no pleasure. It was a just cause.

ZEUS

> And nobody saw you? Nobody went to the Kingdom of
> the Dead
> wearing a picture of your face in his eyes?

ATHENA

> I was invisible – at Odysseus' side.
>
> I lent an unseen hand when he laced the bow,
> bent that obstinate wood into shape.
>
> And I flew when the first arrow was fired,
> guided it smartly into Antinous' hollow throat.
> His eyes stared. Stunned and wordless,
> he buckled at the knees. Blood spouted from his nose.
>
> Eurymachus took the next quill. I carried its flight
> between my finger and thumb,
> felt it shatter the cage of his ribs,
> tear into his hollow chest.
>
> Then I stood behind Telemachus' bronze-headed spear,
> and when timid Amphinomus pleaded for his life
> I drove it home into his hollow lungs.
>
> I had a silent hand in every suitor's death.

ZEUS

It's how justice should be: an invisible, silent force.

ATHENA

And like love too. Love should be the same.

ZEUS

Come here.

ATHENA

My father . . .

ZEUS

You have a speck of blood on your face.

ATHENA

I'll . . . go and wash.

ZEUS

Wait, Athena, you have one more task.

It's night-time on Ithaca.
Look, curtains are drawn in the bed-chamber of husband
    and wife.

Give those lovers the longest night of their lives.
Go to the dawn in the east and hold it back by its edge.
Don't let darkness roll up its blanket just yet.
Don't let the morning saddle its clattering horses to the
    sun.

There'll be other days. And more tragedy for that house, I
    expect –
no hero ever goes quietly into old age.
But let them have their night of all nights.
In privacy. Out of sight.

Now, bring the clouds together in gentle thunder over the
earth
and close this human story from our God-like eyes.

Thunder reverberates over Ithaca.